KILNED
AT THE
CERAMIC
SHOP

KILNED
AT THE
CERAMIC
SHOP

A
BRADDOCK
MYSTERY

DONNA CLANCY

LEVEL
BEST BOOKS

Author Photo Credit: MC Photography

First edition

ISBN: 978-1-68512-593-6

Cover art by Level Best Designs

This book was professionally typeset on Reedsy.
Find out more at reedsy.com

I lost my mom on September 3rd, 2022. She said a prayer every night that I would get a book deal and be traditionally published. She missed being here to celebrate with me by two months, but I know she is doing a happy dance up in heaven.

Praise for Kilned at the Ceramic Shop

"A well-crafted plot that keeps you guessing until the final reveal."—author Holly Quinn, the Handcrafted Mystery series

Chapter One

"This is going to be a boring summer," Tammy muttered, sitting in her car, peering through her binoculars. "There isn't a single person in the shop under sixty years old."

A tap on the window next to her head made her jump. She looked to her left and saw a uniform. Ducking down slightly so she could see the face above the uniform, she smiled when she recognized an old classmate from high school, but it was obvious from the scowl on his face he didn't recognize her. He made a motion for her to roll down her window.

"Zeke? Zeke Peters? It's me, Tammy Wright."

"Tammy! Last I knew, you were living in New York and writing mysteries."

"I was up until yesterday."

"What are you doing sitting in your car spying on your aunt's ceramic shop? Three shop owners in the plaza called in reports because they thought you were staking out the place to rob it."

"No, I'm not robbing it. In fact, I'll be working there this summer. My aunt's arthritis has become so bad she can't lift the molds or load the kilns anymore."

"Before my mom left for Florida, she told me your aunt's hands were getting pretty bad," Zeke confirmed. "You didn't answer my question. Why are you watching the shop?"

"I was checking out the customers. I came back to a quiet small town from a bustling city, and it looks like most of my aunt's customers are her age. I left what social life I did have back in New York City."

"You've been gone a while, and this quiet town, as you call it, has changed quite a bit. We now have chain stores, franchise restaurants, and a two-story mall on the edge of town. Braddock is not the little backwoods place you left right after graduation."

"Sounds like it's not the same as when I left. Anyway, I figured I could do my writing anywhere, and my aunt has no one else to turn to for help. I just wish there were people more my age who frequented her shop."

"There is. She has ceramic classes for all ages. Today is Friday, and it's senior citizen's day. Anyone aged sixty and above gets a ten percent discount. My mom used to be here every week to socialize and work on her various projects, which turned into Christmas presents for everyone."

"That would explain why all the customers are older," Tammy replied.

"Actually, I'm glad you're here. I worry about Clara and her shop. Do me a favor and pull across the street into the parking lot of the Idle Chat. You're spooking people with your covert actions," he requested, smiling.

"I will, and it was nice to see you again, Zeke."

"You, too, Tammy. Maybe once you're settled, we can grab a cup of coffee, and I can catch you up on the way it is around here now."

"I would enjoy that, thank you," Tammy replied, starting her car.

She watched him in her rear-view mirror as he walked away. He was as good-looking as he had been in high school, but back then, he was just another friend in their circle. His deep green eyes still sparkled, and his handsome face hadn't changed, only matured slightly. And he must have been working out because he was all muscle and not a bit of fat.

He entered the herb shop right behind her. The shop owner must have been one of the ones who called in to report her sitting there. In a way, it was nice the other locals were watching out for her aunt and protecting her from any wrongdoing. That part of the small-town vibe of Braddock hadn't changed.

There were no available spaces in the small parking lot behind the ceramic shop, so Tammy parked on the side of the road, running adjacent to the business. She got out, stretched her legs, and locked and alarmed her car. Chuckling to herself, she remembered she was back home and not in the city anymore, so there was no need to secure her vehicle.

She entered the shop and stood in the compact lobby, looking around. Not having been there since the summer she graduated from high school seven years ago, not much had changed. Triple rows of shelves in front of the two bay windows displayed finished pieces that were for sale. The small counter holding the cash register was straight ahead of her. A well-stocked area of paints, glazes, tools, and anything else needed to complete a ceramic project was stacked neatly on floor-to-ceiling shelves behind the counter.

The fact the register sat unguarded close to the front door bothered her. A thief could enter the shop, clean out the cash, and be gone before anyone even noticed. The first thing she would do would be to put a small bell on the front door to announce its opening and closing.

"Clara! You have a customer out here needing your help," one of the ladies announced as she passed the front area on her way to the main classroom.

"I'll be right there," a voice replied from somewhere inside the shop. "Let me wash my hands."

"It's just me, Aunt Clara!"

"Tammy! You are a welcome sight," her aunt exclaimed, bustling toward her to wrap her in a bear hug. "You get more beautiful every day. What's it been? Ten years now?"

"It's only been seven years," her niece replied.

"I know you're a big-time author now, but that's still too long in between visits. I'm so grateful you are going to be here to help me this summer. My business triples with the tourists, and last year, I had an awful time keeping up with the pouring and firing. And now, with my arthritis, it's even harder."

"While I'm here, all you'll have to worry about is teaching the classes. I'll do all the heavy lifting and unloading of the supplies. I better not catch you trying to lift a bucket of slip or anything else over a couple of pounds."

"Things are going to be so much easier for me with you here."

"I do need at least three days off a week to get some writing done."

"I've worked out a pouring and firing schedule for the shop. I made you a copy so you could look it over and make any changes you need to make. It's on the counter next to the register."

"About that. Do you realize anyone could walk in off the street and rob you? We need to install a bell on the door to alert us to anyone entering the lobby," Tammy suggested.

"You can tell you are a city girl now," her aunt said, laughing. "I've been here twenty-six years and never had a problem."

"Times are changing, and with all the tourists you don't know coming into the shop during the summer, you need to be careful."

"True. I guess a little bell wouldn't hurt," she agreed. "Enough about that. Are you all settled in at the cottage? You did get the key I mailed to you?"

Clara owned a beautiful log cabin built on eight acres, a little over two miles away from the shop. On the back end of her property was a good-sized, year-round, three-room cottage. A full bathroom, a bedroom, and a room that was a combination kitchen and living area provided a decent amount of space for one person to live there. As part of the agreement for Tammy coming to help her aunt, she could live in the cottage, rent-free, for as long as she was there.

"I just got in from the city. The moving truck that was supposed to pick up my storage pod showed up late, and then I had to wait for the property owner to sign off on my apartment so I could get my security deposit back."

"The city sounds so complicated," Clara stated, having never lived anywhere but Braddock her whole life.

"Not really. It's the same procedure for anywhere you rent. It will be a pleasant change not to have people banging on my walls and ceiling," Tammy admitted. "The quiet may drive me crazy at first, but it will be good for my writing in the long run."

"The crickets chirping and coyotes howling at night will make up for the lack of your city noises," Clara laughed.

"I'm going to the cottage and unpack my car. I'll come in tomorrow to relearn the layout of the shop and get my feet wet pouring a batch of greenware. If that's okay with you."

"Sounds good. I have a list of items I need for customer orders. There's only an hour before we close for the day and then I have food shopping to do. Do you want to come to the cabin for supper?"

"No, thank you. I'm going to do a little shopping on my own once I empty the car. Then I'm going to go to bed early. It's been a long day," her niece replied. "Besides, I haven't been to The Brown Bear Café since I left, and I could really get into one of their messy, overstuffed Reuben sandwiches right now."

"The café is still there. All the appliances were turned on yesterday, and the refrigerator should be cold enough to fill. I guess I'll see you tomorrow then. And, Tammy, thank you again," her aunt said, hugging her niece a second time. "You are saving my ceramic shop from an ultimate demise."

"Excuse me?"

"I'll explain tomorrow," she replied, running off to help one of her customers.

That was weird. What did she mean by that?

Five minutes later she arrived at the place she would call home for the next five months. It was more like a smaller version of her aunt's log cabin than a cottage you would expect to see on the beach. A porch with two rocking chairs and hanging plants ran along the front of the building. In time, Tammy would replace one of the chairs with a patio set so she could write outside in the fresh air on her days off.

A shed had been built on the side of the house to secure trash barrels as bears would be there each night for a late-night supper if they weren't under lock and key. The yard was neatly manicured, and a walkway of colorful flagstones led to the porch. Tammy pulled a key out of her purse.

As she opened the front door, she could immediately smell the wood fragrance of the wall and ceiling logs. The cottage had been empty for almost two years, but her aunt had a cleaning company come in and do a thorough once-over of the place prior to her niece's arrival.

Stepping in, she found herself in a fairly large space comprised of the living room and a small kitchen. A colonial blue loveseat and a black recliner were facing a good-sized television hanging on the wall above the brick fireplace. Two end tables completed the layout. An oval braided rug covered the living room floor.

She tossed her purse and computer on the loveseat. Moving to the kitchen, she noticed everything she needed was already available to her. Tammy opened the refrigerator and stuck her hand inside. It was cold enough for the groceries she would purchase. The kitchen, done in bright yellows and oranges, was not really Tammy's taste in décor, but it would be okay for the summer.

She looked around for a coffee maker, and there was none. Coffee was a necessity for the writer and part of her morning routine. Foregoing checking out the rest of the place until later, she emptied the back of her car instead. Hoping the five and dime was still open in town, she locked up and headed out on her quest for a coffee maker.

Walking around Roberts' Five and Dime was like going back in time for Tammy. Not much had changed in the last seven years, not even the old registers. When she was growing up, her mother would bring her to the store to do their Christmas shopping, and although there were more modern technological items on the shelves now, the rest of the store still fit the bill as an old-fashioned five-and-dime. She found her coffee pot and went to stand in line at the only open register.

Tammy knew many of the people who walked by her, but they didn't recognize who she was. Leaving the town at nineteen years old for a writing career in New York City, her mom and dad remained in town for just over a year after she left.

Both her parents were originally from Texas. They moved the family to Maine when their daughter was four years old. Aunt Clara needed help to take care of Tammy's grandfather, whose health was failing. The family stayed after his death so their daughter could graduate with her lifelong schoolmates.

"Next!" the clerk yelled, breaking Tammy's train of thought.

She set her item on the counter and took out her charge card. An older man walked up, stood next to the cashier, and stared at her.

"Tammy Wright, as I live and breathe. What brings you back to town?"

"Hello, Mr. Roberts. I am surprised you remember me," she said, smiling.

"I never forget a face, no matter how long it has been since I last saw it," he boasted. "I was so sorry to hear about your mother passing. She was so young."

"It was quite a shock to all of us. I don't think my dad has ever got over losing her to that drunk driver. He's still in Texas with his side of the family."

"Have you seen your Aunt Clara?"

"I did earlier today. I am going to be working at the Idle Chat this summer."

"I always loved that name, Idle Chat Ceramic Shop. My wife, God rest her soul, loved to go there to catch up on all the town gossip. While she was alive, she went there every Friday for Senior's Day and would come home to tell me all she had learned during class, and I'm not talking about the ceramic lessons," he said, chuckling. "I never realized how busy this little town was behind the scenes."

"Back then, things were never as they seemed," Tammy agreed.

"I am so glad you will be with your aunt for the summer. Clara would never admit it, stubborn woman that she is, but she must be afraid of those men who are trying to bully her into selling her shop and land. Well, it was nice to see you again, and don't be a stranger," he said, patting her hand. "And say hi to your dad for me the next time you talk to him."

"I will, and it was nice to see you again, too."

There seems to be more going on at Idle Chat than my aunt is telling me.

Tammy only intended to pick up basics at the grocery store, the most important being coffee, coffee filters, and sugar, but she managed to fill the whole cart with just-in-case items before she finished shopping. She hadn't checked the bathroom before she left and didn't want to be caught without any toilet paper once she had settled in for the night.

Her final stop before returning home was The Brown Bear Café.

She was glad to see her favorite sandwich was still on the menu and requested a Reuben with a side of extra crispy fries to go. The aroma of the corned beef filled the interior of the car, which made her stomach growl, so she swiped French fries out of the bag to hold her over until she arrived home and could dive into the full meal. Tammy hadn't eaten a thing since early morning when she had coffee and a bagel before leaving the city.

The frozen items were set into the freezer, but the rest of the groceries would wait until after she ate. Unwrapping the sandwich, she dug in. The sauce ran over her fingers and down her arms with every bite she took of the over-stuffed sandwich. Breaking open a new roll of paper towels to keep up with the mess the sandwich was creating, she was thoroughly enjoying her first meal in her new house.

As she ate, Mr. Roberts's words came back to haunt her. At least now she had an inkling about what her aunt meant when she said the shop's ultimate demise. She decided it would be the first thing she discussed with her the next morning.

Pouring herself a glass of wine after her meal, she settled into the recliner to watch television. Sometime between the murder happening and the end of the show, Tammy dozed off. She didn't move to her bed until the frenzied howling of the coyotes in the woods behind her cottage woke her up in the wee hours of the morning.

Chapter Two

It was a little after nine when Tammy rolled out of bed. She had always been an early riser and was usually out of bed by six, but the previous day must have taken more out of her than she thought. Staggering to the kitchen, she was ready for her morning cup. The start time on the coffee clock had been set for six-thirty, so the coffee was a little stronger than she normally liked as it had been sitting on the hot plate for almost three hours. She poured it out and made a fresh pot.

Hearing the birds chirping, which she had never heard in the city, she ventured outside with her coffee and sat in one of the rocking chairs on the front porch. The surrounding bushes were alive, with small birds flying in and out. From where she was sitting, she could see small nests tucked inside on the branches, mostly hidden under the cover of the leaves.

Tammy sat back, drinking her coffee, and enjoying the natural activities of country living. A couple of squirrels chased each other across the front yard fighting over a pinecone the bigger squirrel had in his possession. Three chipmunks were playing a game of tag. Two wild turkeys were on the far end of the yard, scratching at the dirt and looking for food. She decided the next time she was in town she would pick up a couple of bird feeders, seed, and some cracked corn for the turkeys.

As she rocked, she closed her eyes and started running ideas through her mind for her next book. She never really set her outlines down on paper. She was a pantser, not a plotter. Pantsers wrote by the seat of their pants letting the story go where it needed to go. Sometimes she knew who would be murdered, but the why had to come to life in the words as the story unfolded.

Out of coffee, Tammy went inside to refill her mug and headed to the shower. The ceramic shop opened at eleven and if she hurried, she could be there to talk to her aunt before any customers arrived. She wanted to know firsthand what was going on with this bully who was pushing her aunt around.

Throwing on an old pair of jeans and a faded tee after her shower, she looked in the mirror at herself. The jeans showed off her slim figure which had been hidden under multiple layers of work clothes she had worn over the last seven years. It was a definite change from the three-piece suits she wore at the publishing house. In the city, she wouldn't have been caught dead outside the confines of her apartment in this outfit and she had totally forgotten how much more comfortable sneakers were instead of heels.

I could get used to this again.

Grabbing her cell phone from its charger and sliding it into her back pocket, she hid her laptop under the couch and left for her first day of work at the ceramic shop. While in the car, her agent called to check in and see if her move to the country had been successful.

Paul Zion, her agent of six years, had picked up her first mystery, Evil Hunter. He sold it to a large publishing company in the first week it was out on submission. Her career took off from there, and together, they sold five additional books, solidifying her position as an established author.

Tammy assured him all was well, and she had several new ideas she would be starting to write when not working at the ceramic shop. He requested the first five chapters when she was finished with them and an overall synopsis of the book. She hung up as she reached the shop.

She recognized her aunt's SUV parked alongside the back of the building near the loading dock where the buckets of slip were stocked. Another vehicle was parked sideways behind her aunt's car. Tammy jumped out of her car, leaving the door open, and ran to see what was going on and if her aunt was okay. As she neared the door, she could hear a heated argument ensuing inside.

"What's going on in here? Who are you?" she demanded as she rushed to her aunt's side.

"Who are you?" the man countered.

"I'm Tammy Wright, Clara's niece. Now, I'll ask you again. Who are you, and what are you doing in Idle Chat when it's closed?"

"This is Wilmont Sawyer. He forced his way in here as I unlocked the door," her aunt replied. "He wants my shop and the land it sits on to build a big condo complex and won't take no for an answer that I will not sell to him."

"I'm trying to talk some sense into your aunt. She has a failing business, and I'm offering her good money to bail her out," he announced, glaring at Tammy as he spoke.

"First of all, he's not talking, he is threatening me. He said he will put me out of business by scaring away my customers," her aunt stated, squaring her shoulders now that she had her niece to back her up.

"Have you called the police, Aunt Clara?" Tammy asked, pulling out her cell phone.

"Not yet, Mr. Sawyer wouldn't let me by to get to the phone next to the register."

"Is this how you run your business? You bully old ladies to get what you want? No offense, Aunt Clara. This is not a failing business and it is a beloved spot by many locals. While I am here, you will not step foot on this property again, do you understand?" Tammy warned him. "This land is not for sale, so you better find another location for your stupid condo complex."

"You don't know who you're dealing with, little girl. I always get what I want."

"Is that another threat?" Tammy inquired, stepping forward and dialing her cell phone. "We need the police at the Idle Chat Ceramic Shop, please. Wilmont Sawyer is here threatening myself and my aunt. Thank you."

"You just made a huge mistake," he growled, his face turning bright red and storming out of the shop. "You'll pay dearly for this."

Backing his car up to Clara's, he spun the tires spraying the car with gravel and rocks, smashing the back window in several places. He drove off smiling, very pleased with himself at what he had done. Tammy recorded the whole event on video on her cell phone.

Several minutes later, a cruiser pulled into the lot. Tammy and her aunt were outside surveying the damage to the car.

"Don't tell me, Wilmont Sawyer?" Deputy Zeke Peters asked.

"Yes. And I want charges brought against him for threatening myself and my aunt and for destruction of property," Tammy insisted, showing Zeke the video.

"I don't want to press charges. My insurance will cover the damage to the car," Clara stated firmly.

"Aunt Clara, you can't let him get away with things like this. He knows people are afraid of him, and he won't be held accountable for his actions. You need to press charges, or he will keep threatening you or maybe even do something worse."

"Your niece is right," Zeke said, looking over the damage.

"I'm not afraid of Wilmont Sawyer, but I am afraid for my customers. He said he would scare them away, and I can't take a chance of what he will do to them," she replied. "Maybe I should just sell him the property and be done with it."

"You will do no such thing, but you can sell the property to me. I have the money to fight him, and he will stop going after you."

"That doesn't sound like a bad idea, Clara," Zeke agreed.

"Think about it, at least. I will own the place on paper, but it would still be yours to run the way you always have. Only the attorneys would have to know I own it."

"What if he still goes after my customers?"

"I will hire a full-time security guard who will patrol the property while your customers are here."

"Are you going to press charges, Clara?" the deputy asked.

"If she doesn't, I will," Tammy stated. "I can't stand bullies."

"What if I take out a restraining order on him for my shop and my house?" Clara suggested.

"You can do that, but I would still press charges, so he has to pay for all the damage he did to your car," Peters suggested. "There is no reason your insurance rates should go up because of Sawyer's immature actions."

"Let me think about it tonight, and I promise I will call you with my answer tomorrow, Zeke," Clara replied.

"That's fine. Please consider Tammy's offer to buy the business. It would take a world of weight off your shoulders."

"It would, but I don't know if I could sell it to her with a clear conscience, knowing he would go after her next," Clara said, wringing her hands.

"Have you ever known me to back down from anyone?" Tammy asked.

"No, never."

"Then don't worry about it. Sawyer doesn't have a leg to stand on legally. If anything, he is the one breaking the law to get what he wants, and that doesn't fly with me," her niece stated.

"Please call me tomorrow, Clara, and let me know your decision. It's time this town stood up to Sawyer and his overbearing tactics. Tammy might be the one to lead the way. With the backing of the local police, of course," Zeke said, smiling.

"If she doesn't call you, I will," Tammy replied.

"Either way, I will talk to someone tomorrow. Call me immediately if Sawyer returns," Zeke requested as he opened the cruiser door. "Be careful, ladies."

"Come on, Aunt Clara. We have work to do, and your customer will be here soon," Tammy said, linking her arm in her aunt's. "You go inside, and I'll take pictures of the damage to your car. That way, we have a record of it in addition to the video I took."

Clara disappeared inside to prepare for the day's business. Tammy watched the cruiser pull away, took the needed pictures, and went inside.

"Today is twelve and under day. Wait until you see how happy the kids get when they are creating something. They really get excited when they are making a Christmas present for someone," her aunt said as Tammy joined her inside the main classroom. "Truthfully, I also like Saturdays because we are closed on Sunday and Monday, and I do enjoy my days off."

"That's when I will be catching up on my writing," her niece said. "For now, I am off to the pouring room to get some of the list of customer orders done. It may take me a while to find the molds in the massive collection back there."

"I knew it would be a problem, so I labeled the shelves prior to your arrival. Each shelf is broken down by holiday, animal, housewares and so on. If you can't find something, come get me, and I will help you locate it," her aunt said. "You're right. I do have an overabundance of molds, but after twenty-six years of being in the same business, you couldn't expect me not to."

"This is for you," Tammy said, holding out a small brown bag.

Clara pulled a small bell from the bag and shook it.

"Not too obnoxious. I guess I could get used to it," she admitted.

"I picked it up at the five and dime last night when I was there getting a coffee maker. I'll put it up right now. It will be one less thing we have to worry about. I don't want Sawyer or any of his goons getting in here unannounced."

"I suppose you're right. We do need to protect ourselves and my customers," Clara sighed. "What is this world coming to?"

"I can't answer that. After a while, you'll grow to appreciate the little tinkle and maybe get to like it," Tammy said, taking the bell from her aunt's hand and shaking it. "Do you have a screwdriver around here somewhere?"

"In the drawer under the cash register. That's where all the odds and ends seem to collect."

"Great! After I'm done, I'll be in the pouring room if you need me."

"Before you go, I have something to give you. This is a key that unlocks the front and loading dock doors. I have one, Goodwin Scott has one, and now you have one."

"Who is Goodwin Scott?"

"He is my delivery man. Twice a week, he brings my slip buckets and other supplies and has been doing it for the last eight years. I trust him immensely."

"This is pretty," Tammy replied, taking the key.

"All three keys match. That way I never mix them up with all the other keys I have. Peacocks are my favorite bird, and the key toppers are the swirled colors of peacock feathers," her aunt replied.

"The key will definitely stand out on my key ring."

"That's the idea," Clara said. "I had them made especially for me at the local hardware store."

"Cool! I'm off to rediscover the world of molds and slip," her niece joked. "But first, the bell."

After locating the screwdriver, the little bell attached easily to the top of the wooden door. Tammy opened it to test how loud the bell was, and on the third time, her aunt came into the lobby area.

"I can hear it in the main classroom and in the sink room. I don't know if you will be able to hear it all the way out back."

"That's all right; at least you'll know the door is opening and someone is entering the shop. If there's a problem, you can always yell for me, and I'll be out here in a flash."

"It's time to open for business. My first class begins in fifteen minutes," Clara said, grabbing several cans of paintbrushes. "Today, the kids are glazing their projects for final firing."

"I'll be out to visit once I have the pouring table full."

"You haven't been out back in a long time. I now have four pouring tables," her aunt advised her. "And a long list of greenware I need."

"I guess I'll be busy then," Tammy said, smiling.

Entering the pouring room, she grabbed an apron hanging just inside the door and put it on over her jeans. The room had been rearranged since she had last been there. Four large pouring tables hugged the perimeter of the room. Buckets of slip had been delivered and were piled three high along the entire far wall near the loading dock door.

Grabbing a full bucket of the cold, grey, slimy substance, she set it next to the largest of the four slotted tables. Placing an empty bucket under the hole at the lower end of the table to catch the runoff when the mold was tipped upside down to drain the excess slip out, she was ready to start.

She walked up and down in front of the shelves, pulling smaller molds which were on the list. When she had pulled enough to fill the first table, she checked the rubber bands surrounding each mold to make sure it was securely closed, and the slip would not leak out of the seams. Filling each one to the top, she waited until a thin wall had formed against the inner mold

15

wall telling her they were ready to be flipped. Her back and arms ached from lifting the buckets and emptying the full molds.

I am so out of shape. Sitting behind a computer for seven years has made me soft.

Tammy had filled three tables when her aunt came in to see if she wanted some lunch. Her niece declined the offer and said she was going to work through lunch so she could finish the list of greenware needed.

"Take a quick break and wipe your hands. This came in the mail today, and you need to read it," Clara said.

"What is it?" Tammy asked, cleaning her hands on her apron and reaching for the paper.

"It's a letter of offer to buy the shop and the land it sits on," Clara answered, shaking her head.

"He just doesn't give up, does he?"

"It's not from Wilmont Sawyer. It's from Flashpoint Realty."

"Are they local?" her niece asked, looking over the offer.

"Their office is located in the new mall on the edge of town."

"I wonder if Sawyer knows he has competition," Tammy said. "It says here they want to build individual homes and not condos on the land."

"I don't want to sell to anybody. Can't they understand that and leave me alone?"

"Who owns Flashpoint Realty? I can't read the signature on the offer."

"I couldn't read it either. I looked in the phone book, but it was a small ad and had no names listed for contacts."

"Hold on a sec."

Tammy took out her cell phone and searched for Flashpoint Realty.

"It says here someone named Toby Brown owns the company. Do you know him?"

"Not personally, but I have heard of him. He owns the bowling alley in town."

"He must know Sawyer wants the property and is trying to beat him to it," Tammy surmised. "Speaking of Sawyer, have you called Zeke yet to press charges?"

"Not yet. I am afraid he will do something to one of my customers if I do. I would never forgive myself if any of them got hurt because of me," she answered, sighing deeply.

"Aunt Clara, that's what he is counting on, your fear. This needs to stop here and now. His reign of terror must come to an end in this town. I will press charges if you don't want to do it, but it does need to be done."

"I'll fight my own battles with that dreaded man. I'll call Zeke right now and not wait until tomorrow," she said, leaving for the front office.

Tammy should have known from past experiences that no one would push her aunt around and get away with it. Clara Beale was born and raised in Braddock and was one tough woman. As harsh as the winters could be in northern Maine, her aunt adjusted to every changing season and even learned to attach a plow to her truck to keep her own road and driveway clear for traversing. She chopped a lot of her own wood for the cold winter months and even learned to shoot a gun to chase away unwanted wild animals from her property. No one messed with Clara Beale.

Never married, she had always lived on only what she could earn herself. Clara opened the ceramic shop to create the year-round income that she needed to survive. Fed up with the way things were being run in the town, she ran for selectman and won. Twelve years later, she was still on the board and highly respected by most of the locals.

Tammy finished filling the fourth pouring table and hung up her apron. She looked around the room and knew she had accomplished a good morning of work. Moving into the kiln room, she scanned the shelves holding the items that needed to be fired. Within an hour, she had the two smaller kilns loaded, one with greenware and one with glazed pieces. She left the big floor kiln empty as she knew there would be several large ceramic Christmas trees and their bases that would have to be fired and would require its larger size.

It had been a long time since she fired a kiln, and she couldn't remember the correct cone she needed to insert before starting the firing process. Deciding to verify which one she needed and not just guess; she went looking for her aunt.

Entering the lobby area, she saw Deputy Peters and another uniformed man she didn't recognize. She walked up to the group.

"Tammy, this is Sheriff Harry Becker. Sheriff, this is my niece, Tammy Wright, who has come to help me for the summer," Clara announced. "She was the one who talked me into pressing charges against Wilmont Sawyer."

"She did, did she? I want your aunt to think about what she may be opening herself up to by pressing charges," the sheriff said. "Sawyer is no one to fool around with, let alone make him mad at you. He's got a mean streak as wide as Niagara Falls."

"As I explained to my aunt, men like Sawyer feed off people's fear. He must be stopped. Are you not willing to enforce the law around here?" Tammy asked, hands on her hips.

"I am NOT afraid of Wilmont Sawyer if that's what you're insinuating. I WILL do what needs to be done. What concerns me is there are only so many of us working each shift, and we can't be here twenty-four-seven guarding your aunt and her customers from Sawyer and his men," the sheriff explained, miffed she was questioning his authority.

"I have already talked to a security company in the adjacent town, and they are sending over three men I can interview for a job guarding the shop and everyone in it while Idle Chat is open."

"And Tammy has other things in the works to help take the stress off Clara," Zeke added. "I love the bell, by the way. It's great protection from anyone entering the shop unannounced."

"That was my niece's idea, too," Clara replied.

"Okay, I'll go file the charges against Wilmont Sawyer and serve him," Sheriff Becker said. "Clara, please be extra careful when you close tonight."

"I'll be here with her. The shop is closed the next two days, but I will be periodically checking in to make sure nothing is amiss."

"You be careful, too," the sheriff warned, wagging his finger at Tammy. "Wilmont Sawyer is a dangerous man. So far, he has been extremely careful in his dealings, but one of these days, he will slip up, and I will get him. Good day."

"I'll be right back," Tammy said, hurrying out the door to catch up with the sheriff before he left.

18

"Sheriff Becker, I want to apologize to you. I didn't mean to insinuate you couldn't or wouldn't do your job regarding Sawyer. It infuriates me he thinks he can do whatever he wants and get away with it, especially when it comes to bullying my aunt. I had to deal with many people in New York who acted the exact same way and thought I was escaping their kind by coming back here."

"Apology accepted. There are a lot of good people in this town, but there is always one bad apple if you know what I mean. Just watch over your aunt for me. The station is twenty minutes away, and we might not be able to get here as fast as she needs us to. Sawyer didn't make his millions by being a nice person and caring about who or what he destroyed in the process. He won't take his anger out on you; he will go after Clara because she is the more vulnerable one."

"There won't be a second she will be here that I won't be," Tammy assured him.

"Good, because with her filing charges, it's only going to get worse," he said, getting in his cruiser.

"Thank you for caring about my aunt the way you do," she said as he closed the car door.

He gave her a thumbs-up and drove away. Coming through the door, Tammy could hear her aunt explaining to one of the mothers of her children's class why the police were there. Upset, it was Sawyer who Clara was defying, she informed the shop owner that her child would not be returning after today out of fear that something might happen while they were there. The mother returned to her son, and they left shortly after.

"It's already starting. Once word gets out, I won't have any more customers," Clara stated, wringing her hands.

"Don't you worry, Aunt Clara. Everything will be fine, I promise," Tammy said, hugging her. "You'll have the Idle Chat until YOU decide you want to retire."

"That may be earlier than I was planning on, I'm afraid."

"You go take care of your students. I have a phone call to make."

She placed a call to her financial advisor. He was out of the office, but his

19

secretary promised to give him her message as soon as he returned from his meeting. It was almost closing time, and Tammy hadn't asked her aunt about the firing cones yet. Clara pulled out a chart and gave it to her niece. Tammy returned to the back room, set the proper numbered cones into the firing pins, and turned on the kilns to fire overnight.

From a distance, she could see her aunt standing at the counter, saying goodbye to her customers. Clara adored the people of this town, and they had embraced her and her business for over twenty-five years. Tammy vowed right then and there to keep the shop open no matter what she had to do. She watched as her aunt cleaned out the register, put the money in a deposit bag and then she started to cry.

"What's wrong, Aunt Clara?" Tammy asked. "Please don't cry."

"Three more children won't be returning for Saturday classes," she wept. "Just the name Wilmont Sawyer is going to put me out of business."

"I won't let it happen," Tammy said, assuring her with a hug.

"You know, the funny part is I had an offer to buy this building about three years ago. Zee Campbell wanted to buy the place and turn it into a beauty salon. She made me a decent offer, and I almost accepted it. If I had, I wouldn't be in this position I'm in right now."

"I have a call into my financial advisor, and I'm meeting and interviewing three men here at the shop tomorrow morning, so we will have security guards in place every hour we are open."

"That's all well, but is it any way to have to run a business? I have to guard my customers so they can come to the shop?"

"I know it doesn't seem plausible right now, but things will calm down, I promise. Once Sawyer finds out the shop belongs to me, and he can't push me around, he will move on and find another location."

"All it does is put you directly in the path of his anger instead of me. I don't know if I can do that," her aunt said, drying her eyes and cheeks.

"You have the next two days off, and I want you to go home and relax. Have an extra glass of wine and soak in the sunshine putzing around in your garden. I will come in and check on the shop, so you don't have to worry," Tammy said.

20

"Oh, I'll worry," her aunt insisted as she locked the door. "Please be careful. I didn't ask you to come back and help me for you to get hurt."

"I promise I'll be careful. Now scoot, and I'll see you Tuesday morning."

After her aunt drove off, she checked all the doors to make sure they were locked. Satisfied everything was secure; she left for home to get some writing done before she had to return to the shop in the morning.

On the way home, Tammy stopped at the feed and grain store to pick up several different types of bird feeders, some suet, and seed. The next morning, while she enjoyed her first cup of morning coffee, she scattered the feeders around the front and side yards and filled them with a variety of food. Refilling her coffee, she sat on her front porch to watch as the birds and squirrels discovered their new food sources.

Before she realized it, she had been sitting there for almost an hour, enjoying the activity going on around her. Hating to leave her little sanctuary, but knowing that she had to, she went inside to shower.

Driving to the shop, she was grateful the men had agreed to meet with her even though it was Sunday. She wanted whoever she hired to start work on Tuesday. Maybe she would hire all three and have them work shifts around the clock so the shop itself, while closed, and the customers who were there while it was open, would be protected.

She pulled into the parking lot at ten forty-five. The first interviewee would arrive at eleven, which gave Tammy a small amount of time to check the building and make sure all was well. Walking up onto the loading dock, she noticed the door was slightly ajar.

This is not good.

As quietly as she could, she pushed the door open far enough for her to slide through. Tammy noticed a new order of slip had been delivered. She relaxed a little, thinking maybe the delivery man had left the door open by accident. Then she saw it. A blood trail leading from the newly delivered buckets into the kiln room. She walked slowly, being extremely careful not to step on any of the blood.

Entering the room, she stopped at the door, looking for where the blood trail led. It ended at the base of the large kiln. Tammy didn't remember closing the lid the day before when she left work. She lifted the cover and let it slam back down. Running out of the building, she stopped on the back dock and called for help.

Chapter Three

"Nine-one-one. What is your emergency?"

"I need the police to come to the Idle Chat Ceramic Shop. I found a body," Tammy stammered.

"Is the person breathing?"

"I don't know, but I don't think so. I think he's dead."

"Do you know who it is?" the dispatcher asked.

"I'm not sure. I think it might be Goodwin Scott, our delivery driver. I see new supplies, but I don't see his truck parked anywhere."

"Don't touch anything. I have the police on the way. Do you have a car there?"

"Yes, I do."

"Good. Please lock yourself in your car and wait there until the police arrive," the dispatcher advised. "I will stay on the phone with you until they get there."

Two cruisers flew into the parking lot, lights and sirens blazing. Sheriff Becker and his son, Deputy Phillip Becker, exited the front car. Two other deputies Tammy had never seen before joined the group from the second car.

"What's going on?" the sheriff asked.

"I came here this morning to meet with the guys I am interviewing for the security jobs, and I noticed the loading dock door was ajar. I entered the shop, walked about six feet, and saw the blood leading into the kiln room."

"Is that where the body is?" Becker asked.

"Yes. The large kiln was closed, and I didn't leave it like that when I left.

So, I opened it. I only saw the top of the head before I let the lid slam closed and came out here to call the police."

"Patterson, Collins, go check it out," the sheriff ordered.

"Did you touch anything?"

"The kiln handle, but my fingerprints will already be on it because of working yesterday," Tammy replied.

A car pulled into the lot. The driver sat in his car staring out the window. "Stay here."

Tammy watched as the sheriff walked to the vehicle, had a short conversation with the man whose facial expression changed to one of fear. He started the car and drove off.

"He was one of the guys looking for a security job. I told him the interviews were not going to happen today and after I told him why, he said to tell you he was withdrawing his application."

Collins exited the building, shaking his head.

"Goodwin Scott is dead. It looks like he was hit on the back of the head with this," he stated, holding up an evidence bag with a piece of a kiln shelf in it that was splattered with blood. "I called the M.E., and he will be here shortly."

Zeke Peters came flying into the parking lot and screeched to a stop next to the cruiser. He jumped out of his truck and ran to Tammy's side.

"Geez, man," the sheriff said. "Do you have to drive like that?"

"I heard there was a body found at the ceramic shop. I see Tammy is all right. Please tell me it's not Clara," he answered.

"It's not. It's the man who delivers Aunt Clara's supplies."

"Goodwin Scott? He doesn't have an enemy in the world. Who would want to kill him?" Zeke asked.

"I can tell you who," Tammy stated.

"I think he was making his delivery, and as he leaned over to put the buckets down, someone came up from behind and whacked him in the head," Collins replied. "There's pieces of the shelf used to hit him on the floor near the buckets. The body is still warm so it couldn't have happened too long ago."

"My aunt is going to be heartbroken. She is going to blame herself for this;

I know she is," Tammy said, frowning. "This will break her. She'll probably sell the property to Sawyer now so no one else gets hurt."

"Speaking of," Zeke said. "Clara just pulled in, and she doesn't look very happy."

"Please tell me it's not true. I was at church and heard people talking." she choked out as she approached the group. "Please, tell me it's not Goodwin."

"I am so sorry, Aunt Clara. Yes, it's Goodwin," Tammy replied. "Someone attacked him when he was making his delivery."

"That's it. I'm closing the shop before anyone else gets hurt. Sawyer said he would force me out of business, and what better way to do it than by killing someone I loved as my own family?"

"Let's not be hasty, Clara. You don't know it was Sawyer. We're going to talk to him right now and see what he knows about this," the sheriff advised her.

"It doesn't matter what he says. The damage has been done, and the shop is now closed," she insisted. "I'll be at home if anyone needs me. I have to figure out how I am going to apologize to Goodwin's mom for what happened to her son."

"Aunt Clara, it wasn't your fault. You have nothing to apologize for. Please, calm down. I will stay here and take care of what needs to be done."

"Oh, but it WAS my fault. I had the nerve to stand up to Wilmont Sawyer, which no one has ever done before. And this is the result."

"It may have been a robbery, you don't know. The police will figure this out," Tammy replied.

"I'm off duty today, so I will stay here with your niece. We'll get who did this to Goodwin, Clara, don't you think we won't," Zeke stated.

"Go home now and I'll stop by later to check in on you. I'll visit with Mrs. Scott and tell her what happened to her son," the sheriff said.

The coroner's vehicle pulled up to the back of the shop. Perry Williams, the M.E., and his assistant, Wendy Finder, crawled down out of the wagon, stopping to put on rubber gloves before they approached the sheriff. They spoke in hushed voices so Clara wouldn't hear what was being said before they grabbed their kits and entered the crime scene.

The sheriff was genuinely concerned for her aunt and was trying to shield her from any more pain. Tammy was witnessing what she missed living in New York City; compassion and caring for another human being. In the city, most people didn't even know their neighbor's names.

"Clara, you need to leave. I don't want you here when they bring Goodwin out," the kindly sheriff said, putting his arm around her shoulders. "I will let you know as things progress. Any questions we have we can ask Tammy. Are you okay to drive?"

"I'm fine. Please get whoever did this, Harry. I beg you," Clara mumbled as the sheriff escorted her to her car.

"We will, I promise."

He returned to the group, and they watched the distraught woman drive away. As soon as her aunt was out of sight, Tammy's attention turned to what was happening in the shop. As a mystery writer, she had written about murder and the investigations that eventually solved it, but this was the real thing. She saw flashes going off as they took pictures of the crime scene. Evidence bags had been filled and taken to the M.E.'s wagon. Finally, she watched as a gurney was wheeled inside.

Minutes later, the same gurney was escorted out of the building, except this time, it had a black body bag strapped on it. This was not how she felt, or her characters felt when she wrote her books. She was sick inside, knowing the dead person was a family friend her aunt had known when he was alive, and he was taken away before his time. Her knees weakened, and she had to sit down.

"Are you okay?" Zeke asked as she sat down on the grass.

"Yeah, I guess. It's just, it's nothing like what I write in my books. The feelings go so much deeper."

"Maybe you should spend a few days with me at work and get some real-life experience in the world of crime. Dead bodies are something you never, ever get used to seeing."

"I guess not," Tammy replied, watching them load the gurney into the back of the wagon. "Will we be able to go into the shop today?"

"I doubt it. They'll keep it cordoned off for a few days in case they have to search for something they may have missed or have to recheck. Why? Do you need something from inside?"

"No, not really. I want to make sure the place is secure before everyone leaves."

"The sheriff will make sure the building is locked up tight," Zeke assured her. "He doesn't want anyone messing with his crime scene."

"Crime scene. In all my aunt's years in business here, I'm sure it's one thing she never would have imagined her ceramic shop being described as in a conversation."

"Times are changing. Sometimes not for the better."

That's what I said to my aunt on Friday. Those exact words," Tammy said.

"I could use a cup of coffee. How about you? I can run across the street while the sheriff is still here and grab us a cup," Zeke offered.

"That sounds so good right now. Black with extra sugar, please."

"I'll be right back. Stay put."

She stood up, walked to the far set of windows, and looked through to the kiln room. The sheriff was talking into his shoulder radio and the other three deputies were scouring the area for clues. Tammy watched them at work, searching every inch of the floor and measuring the blood spatter on the walls and buckets. Zeke returned with their coffees, and she took a long drink.

"Hey, that's hot. Be careful," he warned her.

"The hotter, the better, I say," she smiled, warmed by his concern and the coffee.

They stood there together, watching the scene in front of them. Tammy had never seen real blood spatter, and after the initial shock, she found herself captivated by what they were doing. As the deputies moved around, a glint of light reflected off Collin's wedding ring when he walked under the skylight. It reminded Tammy to check for a ring on Zeke's finger. He was holding his coffee cup in his left hand, and there was no ring to be seen.

That doesn't mean anything. Some guys don't wear their rings to work...but, then again, he's not at work today.

"What?"

"What, what?" Tammy echoed.

"You're staring at me," he said.

"Oh, I'm sorry. Lost in my own thoughts, that's all," she said, fibbing.

What a jerk I am. I'm standing at a murder scene, and here I am, checking for a wedding ring. Could I sink any lower?

The sheriff joined them. Collins and Patterson left in their cruiser.

"They found the delivery truck. It was abandoned with no keys in it. My guys are going to process the scene now."

"Where was it found?" Tammy asked.

"In the woods adjacent to the back of the mall."

"Do they have cameras around the mall?"

"They are in place but not working yet," Zeke answered.

"So much for that idea. Why aren't they working?"

"It's a huge complex, and the company that owns it has been working to install the security system before the start of the holiday season. We are talking about well over five hundred cameras to blanket the entire mall and parking lots. The inside cameras are up and running, but not the outside ones."

"It kind of makes you wonder if the person who did this knew the outside cameras weren't working when he dumped the truck there," Tammy surmised. "Maybe he works at the mall."

"Point taken. We'll check around the area to see if any other businesses have cameras in place that might have caught something. We are done here for today. Do you have keys to lock up?" the sheriff inquired.

"Here you go," she said, handing him her set of keys. "It's the key that looks like a peacock."

"I don't want anyone in here for the next two days. I'll give Clara a call and let her know when she can reopen," the sheriff said, locking the loading dock door.

"Do me a favor, call me first and let me know what's happening. If, and that's an extremely big if my aunt is going to reopen the shop, I would like to come in ahead of her return and clean up the blood and set things right," Tammy requested.

"I'll do what you ask for Clara's sake. She doesn't need to see her shop marred the way it has been," the sheriff replied. "And Tammy, I'm really sorry this happened to your family. This is not how our town functions, it's normally quiet and everyone gets along. Well, mostly everyone."

"My aunt has always loved Braddock and its people. She has always been a trusting soul, and I'm not quite sure how long it will take her to get over this," Tammy said. "She may close the shop permanently, I don't know."

"Give her a little time. Now, I'm going to talk to Sawyer and see what he knows about this. You drive Becker, as I have a few calls to make before we get to the real estate office. Can I keep this key for now in case we have to enter the Idle Chat again?"

"Sure. If I need to get in, I'll use Aunt Clara's key."

The sheriff left. Tammy sat down on the front steps of the shop, and Zeke sat next to her. They were quiet for a good ten minutes, and finally, Zeke spoke up.

"Do you have to wait here for the other two men who you were going to interview?"

"No, I called and cancelled the meetings earlier. I feel so lost right now. Moving here to work and write, I was looking forward to a nice summer at home. I even bought bird feeders for the yard," she rambled.

"If you can't work here right now, why not spend the time writing?"

"I do have a story started. But after seeing a real murder, what I already wrote seems kind of lame."

"You can't think like that. You're a great writer, and instead of putting down your work, you should learn from today and incorporate it into your future writing."

"A great writer? And how would you know, Mr. Peters?"

"I've read all your books. Most times I was first in line at the Book Stop the day your new books were released," he replied. "Your mysteries are great."

"Thank you. I can't believe you read my stories."

"I've read them, and so have a lot of other people around here. At one time, your aunt had all your books displayed in the front window of Idle Chat. She is extremely proud of you."

"You have no idea how happy that makes me."

"Well, Miss Happy, would you like to go get some lunch?"

"I don't know if your other half would appreciate you being seen around town with me."

"If that's a roundabout way of finding out if I have a girlfriend or wife, I don't. Not as of five months ago, anyway. So, how about it? I'm starving."

"Can we go to the Brown Bear Café? I love their food."

"That's my favorite place to eat. I scoff down at least three of their Reubens a week. When you're single, you tend to eat out a lot," Zeke smiled.

"I can't believe this. The first thing I did when I got back to town was to go to the café and get a Reuben with a side of extra crispy fries," Tammy laughed.

"Let's go get ourselves a messy sandwich," he said. "I'll follow you, and you can drop your car off at your house. We can check on Clara and see if she wants anything, and then we can go to the café."

The Brown Bear was quiet, and the couple had their pick of where to sit. They chose a booth near the back. Several locals had stopped to ask for an update on the murder. Zeke declined to answer any questions and referred them to the sheriff.

They ordered identical meals and caught up on each other's lives as they ate. They laughed at each other as the Russian dressing and sauerkraut ran down their hands when they bit into their sandwiches.

"So, what happened five months ago to cause you to be single now, if you don't mind me being nosy," Tammy asked in between bites.

"Do you remember Emily Bosen?"

"Yeah, she was in your class, wasn't she?"

"We started dating our senior year, and we both attended the local community college. After I received my associates, I enrolled in the police academy in Bangor. She was working at Doc Carson's office as his receptionist. Everything was going great until we started to talk about getting married. She decided she didn't want to be stuck in Braddock the rest of her life, and she up and moved to California."

"Excuse me? No warning, she just moved?"

"Oh, she gave me a warning, all right. We were having dinner on Sunday night, and on Monday morning, she left. I haven't heard from her since."

"That's so not right. After all those years together?"

"Yeah, she was gone. Since then, it's been just me and my black lab. It was too quiet around the house after she left, so I visited the animal rescue league and found Blinky, who had been abandoned by his previous owner because he had medical issues. Now, we are inseparable."

"You'll have to bring Blinky over to my house so I can meet him."

"As I live and breathe, it's Zeke Peters and in the company of a female," an elderly woman said, walking by sporting a cane.

"Hello, Mrs. Cotton. How are you doing today?" Zeke asked.

"I was okay until I heard about Goodwin. I used to babysit him when his mother was at work. Such a shame," she said, shaking her head and leaning on the edge of the table. "He was such a wonderful, caring young man."

"Yes, he was a good person," Zeke agreed.

"And who is this?" she asked, pointing at Tammy.

"Hello, Mrs. Cotton. I guess you don't remember me. I'm Tammy Wright."

"Now that you mention it- you do look like Tammy," she said, peering over the top rim of her glasses.

"Is she your new girlfriend?" Mrs. Cotton whispered to Zeke.

"No, we're just having some lunch," Zeke whispered back.

"Oh, too bad. Well, keep trying. The right one will come along," she replied, patting the back of Zeke's hand. "I have to get home and feed my cat."

"Goodbye, Mrs. Cotton. Nice to see you again," Tammy said.

"You too, dear."

"Well, that was embarrassing," Zeke said when she was out of earshot.

"Cut her some slack. She's old and is only looking out for you."

"Problem is, they're all looking out for me. Anyone over the age of eighty is trying to match me up with someone. I guess Braddock has a written rule somewhere in the town books: you have to be married by the time you're thirty," he said, frowning.

"Come on, it can't be that bad."

"Just wait. If you are here any longer than a month, they'll start looking for you, too."

"I don't know how long I'll be here if Aunt Clara decides to close the shop and sell it," Tammy replied. "Today was a major blow to her."

"I know, I could see it in her face," Zeke agreed.

"I sure hope the sheriff finds out something when he questions Wilmont Sawyer. I know he's responsible for this, and I feel like Goodwin's death is more my fault than anyone else's," Tammy sighed. "I was the one who insisted my aunt stand up to the man, and she listened to me."

"It's no more your fault than it is your aunt's," Zeke stated. "The sole responsibility is on the person who committed the crime."

"Then why do I feel so miserable?" she asked.

"Because a decent human being died for no good reason. Anyone who knew Goodwin feels miserable right now," he answered, taking her hand. "I want you to be extra careful, both you and your aunt. You just returned to town, and I don't want anything to happen to you."

"I'll be careful," she said, feeling warm all over that Zeke was looking out for both of them.

"I have a confession to make," Zeke claimed.

"And what would that be?"

"I had the biggest crush on you in school, but it always seemed like you wanted nothing more than to be friends," he said. "And then you left for New York City, so I let it go."

"Seriously? I never noticed. I always thought you and Emily were a thing and never questioned your relationship with her."

"I guess we were. Back then, it seemed it was supposed to be that way, her the head cheerleader and me the captain of the football team."

"You were voted class couple and the homecoming queen and king."

"Kind of dumb, huh? The things which were so important back then seem so small now."

"Not dumb, it was important to us at that time in our lives. We've all grown up and followed the paths we wanted to take, and sometimes, paths bring us back to where we started."

"Do you think if Clara closes the shop, you might stick around for a while," he asked.

"I think I can stick around for at least the summer to see what develops," she said, smiling. "Besides, I may own a business here in town, which would help to lay down some roots."

"And if Clara sells the business to someone else?"

"I will cross that bridge when and if I come to it," she replied. "Right now, I am more concerned for my aunt's well-being. It's her decision and no one else's if she decides to sell and walk away."

"Maybe it would be the best thing for her, as long as it's not to Sawyer."

"She did mention Zee Campbell made her an offer for the shop. I don't think she will sell to anyone right now fearing she would put them in danger. Sawyer has her pretty spooked, and she just might give in to him to protect others," Tammy said sadly.

"The Braddock Police Department will back Clara in whatever she decides to do. Maybe if we catch the killer, your aunt will stay put in the shop."

"That's exactly what I plan to do: catch the killer," Tammy stated.

"You need to leave it to the police. This is not like writing a murder in a novel. This is real life, and you are dealing with real, very dangerous people."

"I won't interfere with your investigation, but I do intend to see what I can figure out on my own."

"Just like Clara, stubborn as all get out," Zeke said, shaking his head.

"I guess it runs in our family."

"Promise me that if you discover something, you will call me and not go anywhere by yourself to confront anyone," he requested.

"I will, I promise."

"Good. Now, I have to go let Blinky out to do his thing. Would you like to stop and meet him, or would you like me to take you home first?"

"I would love to meet him."

Tammy opened her purse to take out her wallet.

"My treat," Zeke insisted.

They left the diner together with many sets of eyes watching them.

Chapter Four

As she refilled her feeders the next morning, the birds sat on the branches above her head, chirping while waiting for their food. It was as if they were saying good morning and thank you to her. Taking an empty coffee can, she filled it with cracked corn and wandered to the back of the property, sprinkling it on the ground for the wild turkeys who hung around in the yard during the day.

Tammy welcomed the fact that it had only been three days and that she was already in love with the small-town living vibe again. Returning to the porch and her favorite rocking chair, she listened to the birds sing while tossing around the pros and cons of staying in the town permanently and not returning to New York. Yes, the city provided more of a social life, a better choice of restaurants, and more upscale stores, but did she really need all that? And the city didn't have Zeke. She might have to stick around just to see if the relationship progressed at all.

Her cell phone chimed inside the cottage. Running to answer it, she fell over the coffee can and almost face-planted into the screen door. She got to the phone just as it stopped ringing. Not recognizing the number on the callback screen, she ignored the call. As she put the phone down it rang again, the call coming from the same number.

"Tammy?" someone whispered. "Are you home?"

"Aunt Clara, is that you?"

"Someone is outside my house looking in my windows," she answered.

"Are your doors locked?"

"Yes, I think so. Oh, I don't know. Can you come over right now?"

"Stay away from the doors and windows. Call 911. I'll be there as quick as I can," Tammy said, running out her front door and grabbing a shovel leaning against her porch.

As she ran across her aunt's backyard, she saw a figure standing outside the kitchen window at the back of the cabin. He was trying to force it open. Tammy let out a yell, startling the intruder, who ran off into the adjacent woods. She followed him, dodging trees and hanging branches, and only stopped when she heard a car start up and drive away. When she arrived back at her aunt's cabin, the sheriff and Zeke were talking to Clara on the front porch.

"Why are you out of breath?" Zeke asked her as she joined them.

"I saw him. He was trying to get in through the kitchen window, so I yelled at him. He took off through the woods, and I chased him, but he got away in a car before I could reach the road."

"Oh, Tammy. Why did you chase him?" her aunt asked.

"Did you see his face?" the sheriff asked.

"Only from a distance. He had long, dark hair and a full beard and was dressed in black jeans and a t-shirt. I'd venture to say he was about six foot and very husky."

"You could tell all that from a distance?" Sheriff Becker questioned.

"Well, he was tall enough to be looking in the window flat-footed, so yes."

"You shouldn't have chased him," Zeke lectured. "What if he doubled back?"

"I had a shovel with me," she answered.

"He still could have hurt you," Zeke said, frowning.

"What bothers me is Clara's car is sitting in the driveway. Whoever it was must have known she was at home and was trying to get in anyway," Sheriff Becker said. "I don't like this at all."

"It definitely wasn't Wilmont Sawyer. This guy was half his age," Tammy stated.

"We talked to Wilmont. Judging by his shock when we questioned him, I don't think he had anything to do with Goodwin's murder."

"I still don't trust him. He could have been faking his surprise," Tammy said.

"He could have, but I've been doing this many years, and personally, I don't think he's that good an actor," the sheriff replied.

"Who else could it be? He's the only one interested in the property," Zeke said.

"No, there are others," Clara announced.

"I need you to make me a list of anyone showing interest in Idle Chat. They all need to be checked out," the sheriff said. "Clara, is there anyone you could stay with until we have this whole thing solved?"

"I will not be chased out of my own home!" Clara exclaimed, mad at the suggestion.

"Sheriff, I'm not even a minute away in the cottage. We can install an alarm system until the person is caught," Tammy suggested.

"An alarm system? Really?" Clara said. "The bell was bad enough, and now this?"

"I feel really strongly about this. Tammy is right. It's either an alarm system or stay with someone else," Sheriff Becker replied. "You can always remove the system when everything is over."

"Or…I could stay here in the spare room," Tammy offered.

"You will do no such thing," Clara said. "I will not be treated like a helpless old lady."

"That's not what anyone is implying," her niece replied. "We want you to be safe, that's all."

"I'll set my own booby-traps, thank you. I can look after myself," Clara insisted.

"Whatever you say, Clara," the sheriff said. "Come on, Zeke. There is nothing more we can do here. Call us if the intruder returns."

"What about the shop? Can it reopen, not that I am going to do it right now," Clara asked.

"I wouldn't advise it. Wait until at least Friday, please. We still have a little more to do there," the sheriff answered. "Tammy, can I speak to you in private, please."

"Before you continue, I want you to know she won't change her mind about anything," she said, stepping out onto the porch.

"I know she won't. I have known Clara for a long time, and she is as stubborn as she is independent. I wanted to tell you we are done at the shop, and you are free to go clean up like you wanted to do. I figured I'd tell your aunt Friday to give you a few days to finish without her knowing."

"I appreciate it, thank you. She needs to walk into her beloved business and see it the way it has always been and not changed by what happened to Goodwin."

"And please don't go chasing any more intruders the way you did. I don't need to deal with two murders in this small town," he advised.

"Second nature, I guess. I have never been one to back away from anything."

"Let me give you my private cell phone number in case you can't get through to the station," the sheriff said. "Oh, and here is your peacock key."

Tammy entered the number into her phone.

"Let me give you mine while we're at it," Zeke said, joining them on the porch.

After they drove away, Tammy went inside the cabin to check on her aunt. She laughed as she entered the kitchen. Clara was staging tin cans on the windowsills. On top of each can was a spoon, perfectly balanced against the glass pane, which would fall if the window was opened. The back door already had a rope strung across it with pots and pans hanging from it.

"This is how we take care of things ourselves," Clara said proudly. "I don't need any expensive alarm system to protect my cabin."

"You're unbelievable, Aunt Clara," Tammy said, amazed at the tenacity of her aunt.

"Don't just stand there, grab some cans and spoons, and alarm my living room windows. Set the cans in each corner of the windows so they are not so obvious from outside."

"This is all well and good, but what happens if an alarm goes off and the intruder starts to come inside anyway?" Tammy asked.

"If anyone is stupid enough to do that, they will have the terrible luck of meeting up with Mrs. Everything."

"Who is Mrs. Everything? Do I know her?"

"Hold on," she said, going into the kitchen and returning with a cast iron frying pan.

"That is Mrs. Everything?' Tammy asked, laughing.

"Yes, it is," her aunt said, waving the black pan in the air. "Appropriately named because I use her to cook everything. I've had this beauty many years and she still is my favorite pan."

"I pity anyone who attempts to come into this house," Tammy stated. "They have no idea who they are dealing with. Let's finish the windows and then string up a warning system for the cellar bulkhead."

An hour later, the entire house was alarmed Clara style, and her niece excused herself to return to her cottage to do some writing. Sitting at the kitchen table, she called her financial advisor, who hadn't returned her call yet. After talking for half an hour, it was decided he would investigate the comparable values for the commercial properties around the Idle Chat and draw up an offer to present to Clara. He deemed it a good investment for Tammy's portfolio as most real estate increased in value over time. Promising to get back to her within the week, he hung up.

The writer spent the rest of the day starting the first draft of her new novel. Two chapters in, she stopped to write the synopsis her agent had requested. Her usual process was to shut off her phone while writing, but decided against it in case her aunt needed her again. Around four o'clock, her phone quacked like a duck, the noise it made when she was receiving a text message.

She looked at the screen for the most recent message. It was from Zeke asking her to join him for Reubens at six o'clock at the Brown Bear. She quickly texted back, saying she would be there. Her mind wandered, happy he wanted to go to dinner with her. Tammy finished the synopsis she was writing and went to shower.

Flipping through the clothes she had brought with her, she settled on a coral-colored summer sweater with black jeans. Most of her closet was professional and not casual. She needed to do some shopping. Tomorrow, she would go to the new mall, and while she was there, she would check out the real estate office that sent her aunt the letter offering to buy Idle Chat.

During dinner, Tammy mentioned the fact she was going to visit the real estate office at the mall the following day. Zeke wasn't crazy about the idea as the police hadn't checked them out yet, and they were on the list of potential buyers. She assured him the mall was a busy spot and she would be perfectly safe. He made her promise to call him when she left there, so he knew she was safe. She agreed.

Zeke followed her home and flashed the headlights at her once as she walked through the front door of her residence. She turned, waved goodbye, and closed and locked the door. It was only eight-thirty, so Tammy sent the synopsis she worked on earlier in the day to her agent, promising to keep him updated. At midnight, she had added another half a chapter to her work in progress and closed her computer to go to bed.

A certified letter had been delivered to Clara's cabin the following morning. A text message had been sent informing Tammy it was from her financial advisor. She was surprised it had arrived so quickly, as he had said it would take about a week for research. Tammy stopped at her aunt's cabin to discuss the contents of the letter with her before she left to go shopping. Clara promised to look over the offer and said she would be ready to discuss it further when her niece returned.

The mall opened its doors at ten. Checking the directory to see where the Flashpoint Realty office was located, she formulated a plan in her mind. She would tell them she was looking to purchase a house in the area and needed help doing so. The business was on the far end of the mall, and no one was in the office when she entered.

Standing there waiting for someone to come out from the back, Tammy could hear two men arguing. She caught the words Idle Chat and listened more closely to what was being said. Managing to pick up words here and there, she heard money, Sawyer, and contracts. Suddenly, it became quiet, and a man, large in stature, appeared before her, staring her up and down.

"Can I help you with something?" he asked.

"I was looking for the owners of the agency," she replied.

"I'm Toby Brown. I own Flashpoint Realty."

"Mr. Brown, I am new to the area and will be looking to buy a house soon. I have a list of very specific things I require for my new residence and am looking for an agent to help me find what I need."

"And you would be?" he asked.

"My name is Tammy Wright. I am an author. Maybe you have heard of me or my books," she answered, trying to sound impressive.

She heard the door to the office slam. Deciding to be direct to see if there would be any other sort of response, she proceeded.

"My aunt is Clara Beale. She owns Idle Chat. Your office sent her an offer to buy her business. She is at odds with Wilmont Sawyer at the present time and suggested I come to talk to you, being the only other realty office in town."

Brown smiled when he heard the latest information regarding Sawyer's stance with Clara. Tammy could almost see the dollar signs ringing up in his eyes.

"Well? Can you help me, or do I need to go elsewhere?" she asked.

"Why don't you have a seat? I will go to my office and get a new client packet. Help yourself to a cup of coffee; it was just made about ten minutes ago."

Tammy attempted to get closer to the hallway leading out back so she could hear what was being said behind the closed door. The two men were talking again, and when the voices ceased, she scurried to stand next to the window overlooking the woods at the back of the mall. Brown eyed her suspiciously when he returned to the reception area.

"You have a beautiful view of the woods instead of looking at dozens of parked cars," she said, trying to sound friendly.

"I guess," Brown shrugged. "Shall we get to work?"

"I have an appointment with my agent in a half an hour. Would it be possible for you to give me the papers you need filled out, and I can do it at my rental while I make my phone calls? I will also include a thorough list of all the items I will require in my new home."

"I don't know," he started to respond.

"Money is no object if I find the house I really want. If you can't work with me, I'll go spend my millions elsewhere," she insisted, trying to catch his attention by throwing around lots of zeros.

"We may be building brand-new homes you can customize any way you like," he replied when he heard she was not afraid to spend a large sum of money.

"And how long would I need to wait?"

"Hopefully, we'll be starting to build in the Fall," he answered. "Meanwhile, take this packet with you, fill out what you can, and bring it back. We can work from there to set a plan in motion for your new residence."

"Thank you," Tammy said, reaching for the packet. "I look forward to working with you. I just hope you can deliver what you say you can."

Tammy exited the office and walked toward the rear entrance of the mall, feeling eyes watching her as she left. When standing at the window inside the realty office, she had seen the yellow police tape still wrapped around a plot of trees on the edge of the woods. She assumed it was where the delivery truck had been abandoned, and she wanted to check out the area.

It seemed too much of a coincidence the delivery truck had been dumped right outside the back door of the realty company that was interested in the Idle Chat property. Someone was either extremely stupid, or they were being made to look guilty of the murder by association.

Walking along the edge of the parking lot near the yellow tape, she took out her phone like she was answering it and talking to her agent. Chatting gibberish into the speaker to keep her lips moving like she was actually talking to someone; she perused the area as she paced. Occasionally she waved her hand in the air like she was frustrated with who she was talking to on the other end.

I should get an award for this performance.

The truck had been removed from the area. She sat down at the concrete parking stop nearest the woods. Keeping the phone to her ear, she stretched out as if she were enjoying the sun shining on her face. Brown was still watching her from the window. Leaning over ever so slightly, she picked up a business card lying on the ground and slipped it into her sneaker.

Finishing her pretend phone call, she slipped her phone into her purse and headed back to the mall to do some shopping. She waved to Brown as she walked by the office door. Entering the first clothes store she came to, she stood behind a hanging rack and pulled the card out of her shoe. It was a Wilmont Sawyer Realty business card.

Why would this be near the area of the truck? His office is clear across town.

She tucked the card in her purse, called Zeke to let him know she was okay and started her shopping. Traveling from store to store, she shopped until she couldn't hold any more bags. When she was finished, she had a new casual wardrobe that would carry her through the entire summer and into the cooler weather. A few of the stores had already started displaying colder weather clothing, and Tammy made a mental note of ones she wanted should she decide to stay in Braddock.

Sitting in her car, she called her aunt to make sure everything was okay at home. Clara assured her nothing out of the ordinary had taken place, and all was quiet. Tammy told her she would be home after she finished food shopping.

Pushing her cart through the meat section, Tammy heard someone giggling behind her. She turned to see Mrs. Cotton pointing at her and commenting to the woman she was standing with at the end of the aisle.

"She's the one," Tammy heard her say. "She's the one who's caught our Zeke's eye."

She smiled at the two women, and they hurried off, knowing they had been caught gossiping.

Some things never change in a small town, and gossip is one of those things.

Cleaning supplies filled half her cart as she would be cleaning the kiln room at the shop the next day to wipe away any traces of Goodwin's murder before her aunt returned. Tammy completed her shopping, making sure she had included two hearty steaks to cook on the grill for her and Zeke, a grill she had to buy first. Purchasing an insulated bag for the perishables, she was good to continue her shopping.

She also needed a patio set for her porch so she could write outside in the fresh air. Figuring Braddock Hardware would have both items she needed, she headed there next.

Tammy knew nothing about grills. Where she lived in her New York City apartment, they weren't even allowed to have a small hibachi on the balcony.

Looking around for someone to help her, she spotted a clerk at the back of the store.

"Excuse me," she said, walking up behind him.

"Tammy! I heard you were back in town," he said as he turned around.

"Stan Perry, how are you?"

"I'm good. I hear you and Zeke are hanging around together."

"Wow! News travels fast around here," she laughed. "We had a friendly dinner together, that's all."

"How can I help you?"

"I need a grill but have no idea which one I should get. I also need a patio set. Do you deliver?"

"We do have next-day delivery. Do you want a charcoal or propane grill?"

"Which do you recommend?"

"Propane is less messy and cooks quicker, but some people like the added flavor the burning charcoal gives to their food. It's up to the individual's taste, I guess."

"Let's go with a propane grill. If I pay extra, can I get it put together and ready to go? I'm not great at reading directions."

"We can assemble it for you. How is Clara doing? We were all so sorry to hear about Goodwin," Stan asked as they walked to the grill displays.

"She's taking his death hard. She feels responsible and said she won't open Idle Chat again because of it."

"It wasn't her fault. If it's anybody's fault, I blame the darn real estate companies around here. Braddock has become quite a busy place and people like Wilmont Sawyer are seeing dollar signs. They are trying to buy up everything and making a lot of people mad in the process."

"What about Flashpoint Realty? Do you know anything about them?"

"Not much. I know Toby Brown is the owner, but word has it there is someone else who fronted the money to start the realty business, a silent partner. Toby owns the bowling alley, but it's not a popular spot. It can't be pulling in enough money to finance a second business venture. I didn't even know Toby had his real estate license. Why do you ask?"

"It seems they are interested in my aunt's property, too. They are competing with Sawyer to purchase it for development."

"That's interesting. I just heard Flashpoint bought the old Grady residence and all the adjacent land. I guess Sawyer has some real competition now, and I bet he doesn't like it one bit."

"The Grady property isn't far away from Idle Chat. If they could get my aunt to sell, they could buy up the property in between and have a huge chunk of land to develop."

"Like I said, I don't know where Toby Brown is getting all this money from to buy all these properties. It doesn't make any sense."

"No, it doesn't."

"So, if you are going to be cooking out a lot, I suggest this grill. It comes with a propane tank and a cover to protect it from bad weather," he suggested, pointing to a black grill.

"I'll take your word for it. As I came into the store, I saw a dark green patio set out front with a glass table, four matching chairs, and a matching umbrella. Is that available to purchase, or is it a sample?"

"We have boxed ones out back, so you'll get a new set never used. Let's go check the schedule to see what time we can get everything delivered to your house tomorrow."

With a delivery time set for ten o'clock the next morning, it would give Tammy plenty of time to complete her work at the ceramic shop later in the afternoon. She was walking out the door when Stan called out to her.

"I don't know if you or your aunt heard or not, but Sawyer has purchased the old, abandoned drive-in on the other side of the street, a mile down from her shop."

"No, we didn't know. It seems the only plot of land left to buy in the area is the plot the Idle Chat sits on."

"Mrs. Cotton, who lives right behind the shop, hasn't caved in yet. She insists she's going to die there, and no one is going to chase her away from the house her husband built for her."

"I hope she doesn't eat those words," Tammy said, sighing.

"Me, too. Say hi to Clara for me and give her my best."

The groceries put away; she strolled over to her aunt's cabin to check in

44

on her. The back door was open, which Tammy thought was odd.

"Aunt Clara! Are you here?"

No answer. Tammy walked around, room to room, looking for her missing aunt, hoping she hadn't fallen and hurt herself. Her aunt's keys were hanging on the hook in the kitchen and her purse was underneath the counter. She could see her aunt's car sitting in the driveway outside the window above the sink.

After checking every room, including the cellar, she went outside and hollered for her aunt while walking towards the woods. She pulled out her phone and called the sheriff.

Chapter Five

Ten minutes later, Sheriff Becker, his son, and Deputy Collins had joined in the search for Clara. They blanketed the woods that surrounded the property. Finding no signs of the woman, they met up in the backyard.

"I just talked to her not an hour ago," Tammy said. "She was fine."

"I don't like this," the sheriff stated. "Clara wouldn't just wander off and not let anyone know where she was going."

"As I crossed the yard, I noticed the back door was ajar. My aunt would never leave it like that as she is allergic to bees and didn't want them in her house."

"Collins, go see if the occupants of the house at the head of the road saw any vehicles entering or leaving the area within the last hour."

Tammy and the remaining two officers reentered the house.

"I checked her purse, and her wallet is still there. It doesn't appear to be a robbery," she stated. "There's only one thing missing besides my aunt. The envelope with the offer I had drawn up to buy Idle Chat."

"Had Clara seen it?" the sheriff asked.

"It arrived this morning by overnight delivery. I came over to discuss it with her before I left for the mall."

"Was Clara open to the idea?"

"I believe so. We talked about her running the shop until she wanted to retire, and then we were going to offer it to Zee Campbell, who is still interested in the property for her hair salon. She had told my aunt she could buy the building and still be paying less each month for a mortgage than the

46

rent they wanted to charge her for a retail space at the mall. We were going to discuss it further when I got home."

"Were all the windows open like they are now?"

"I think so. Why? Do you think someone was listening to our conversation?"

"I believe so, and, truthfully, I think Clara has been kidnapped, so she couldn't sell the shop to you," the sheriff replied. "I need you to stay here in case she shows up or calls. I'm going to talk to Wilmont Sawyer."

"While you're at it, you might want to talk to Toby Brown at Flashpoint Realty. He and Sawyer are both fighting to buy the same properties around town. And before you go, I have something to show you. I'll be right back."

Tammy ran to her cottage to get her purse. When she returned, she gave the sheriff the business card she had found.

"This was near where the delivery truck had been abandoned. I thought it was weird because Sawyer's office is all the way across town," she said.

"And what were you doing over there?"

"I had some shopping to do, but I also wanted to check out Flashpoint Realty as they were involved in the offers to buy my aunt's property."

"You really need to stay out of this. These men mean business and now I'm afraid one of them has taken Clara."

"I went into the office and was very upfront with them. I told them who I was, but I did make up a story about buying a house in the area. When I told him money was no object, he was very quick to tell me his company would be building some brand-new homes very soon. He seemed extremely confident that he would be able to advance with his plans and build his new housing development on my aunt's property."

"We will check his company out thoroughly."

"There's something else you should know. I was at the hardware store this morning, and Stan believes Brown doesn't have enough money to finance all these big deals. He thinks he has a silent partner. And while I was at the realty office, I heard Brown arguing with someone in the back room."

"You sure get around, don't you?" the sheriff said, shaking his head. "Please, just stay here in case Clara calls. We'll check into the rest."

"I will. I was going to the shop to clean it today, but I'll stay put and look around for any other clues to my aunt's whereabouts."

After the sheriff left, Tammy continued to poke around the property outside the cabin. She wasn't exactly sure what she was looking for but kept searching anyway. The mail truck pulled up to the mailbox. Tammy flagged him down.

"Thank you," she said, taking the mail offered to her. "You haven't seen my Aunt Clara walking around anywhere in your travels, have you?"

"No, can't say that I have. Have a good day."

"Oh, Aunt Clara, where are you?" Tammy asked, looking around.

Returning to the cabin, she dumped the mail on the kitchen table and turned on the kettle to make a cup of tea to calm her stomach. Tammy stayed on the porch, mindlessly sipping her apple cider tea and waiting for either her cell phone or her aunt's landline to ring, but both stayed silent.

Zeke's pickup pulled into the driveway. Even seeing her good-looking friend didn't make her feel any better. He got out of the truck and sat down next to her in the adjacent rocking chair. He took her hand.

"I just heard. Any news yet?"

"No, nothing," she replied. "I'm so worried about her, Zeke."

"Sheriff Becker will find her. Most of the town has been alerted, and everyone is looking for her. Collins has been posted at the Idle Chat watching for any suspicious activity."

"The sheriff seems to think someone was listening from outside the cabin to our conversation about my offer to buy Idle Chat. They took Aunt Clara and the contract so she couldn't sign the paperwork."

"Makes sense. These people are playing for keeps and probably figured it would be easier to deal with Clara than with you. I have to say I really admire your aunt. She is one tough lady," Zeke said. "She'll be okay; I just know it."

"I hope you're right," she said.

"Do you want to walk the property and see if we can find anything to tell us what happened to her?" Zeke suggested.

"The sheriff told me to stay close to the cabin in case she called. I don't think she knows my cell number by heart, so the only place she could call would be here on the landline. We have to stay close enough so I can hear it ringing."

"We'll turn the ringer up as loud as it goes and stick it in the screened window at the back of the cabin. Come on, let's try to find your aunt."

After placing the phone in the open window, the couple walked around the yard, looking for anything that could be out of place. Tammy felt better knowing she was not alone.

"They checked the woods heading out to the main road, but they didn't check around my place. Let's head that way first," Tammy suggested. "I'll still be able to hear the phone if it rings."

Two hours went by, and they walked the property, finding nothing. It was like Clara had vanished into thin air. Tammy grabbed her computer from her own place, and they went back to her aunt's cabin. Knowing she would be there for the next few hours or more and needing something to keep her mind occupied, she was hoping to be able to write.

Zeke left as he had an appointment to finish his qualifications on the range for his law enforcement job but promised he would return after he was done.

Tammy opened her computer and stared at the blank screen. All she could think about was her aunt and if she was okay. Not being able to write, she pulled out the packet of papers from Flashpoint Realty and filled out what she could without giving them too much personal information about herself or her finances. Done with that, she wandered around the cabin aimlessly.

"I can't sit here and do nothing, no matter what the sheriff says," she said, looking out the window at her aunt's car in the driveway. "I think I'll pay Wilmont Sawyer a visit."

Placing her computer in a new hiding place at her aunt's cabin, she left for town. When she arrived at Sawyer Realty, the sheriff's car was parked out front. Not daring to interfere with the investigation of the sheriff and not wanting him to know she left the cabin, she decided to go to Flashpoint Realty instead.

Tammy entered the office, and two men were standing at the door of the back office. When they noticed her standing there, the dark-haired man

Tammy had never seen before but that looked vaguely familiar to her hurried into the office and slammed the door. Brown came walking towards her, not looking happy.

"What can I help you with today?" he snapped.

"You know, the more I deal with you, the more I believe I will go out of town to spend my million dollars," she snapped back. "Good day, Mr. Brown."

"Wait, I apologize. It's been a tough week. A few setbacks here and there. I see you have your information with you. Would you like me to go over it with you?" he asked, his demeanor changing when he heard the magical amount of money Tammy was willing to spend.

"I don't know. As much as my aunt doesn't like Wilmont Sawyer, I believe I will check him out and see how I am treated there. This place always seems to be in such an upheaval whenever I come here, arguing and such."

"I'm sure every business has its moments of upheaval, as you call it."

Maybe, but I think I will hold on to this just a little bit longer until I exercise all my options," Tammy said, waving her packet in the air.

"Whatever," he mumbled.

"And just so you know, in a few days from now, I will be the official owner of Idle Chat. So, any more offers of purchase should be addressed to me and not my aunt," she said, watching for a reaction from Brown.

"Duly noted," he said, glaring at her. "When you have made up your mind about which agency you are going to use, let me know. Good day, Miss Wright."

Taking that as an invitation to leave, she did just that.

Retreating to her car, she wished she had listened to the sheriff and stayed put at her aunt's place. Realizing it was too late and she had just made a huge mistake, she started to cry.

What if they have my aunt? Now they are going to think they don't need her alive anymore because she has already signed the sale papers. Me and my big mouth. What have I done?

Moisture streamed down her cheeks as the stress of the day was released with the waterfall of tears. She closed her eyes and wished sometimes she wasn't so headstrong. Wanting to be right all the time was a major fault of hers, and she knew she had to work on changing that.

Then she remembered they had taken the envelope containing the sale offer with them when they took her aunt. Maybe they would know she was bluffing, and it would buy her aunt a little more time if it had been Brown and his friend who took Clara.

A light tapping on her window made her open her eyes. The sheriff was signaling her to step out of her car.

"Are you okay?"

"I did something really stupid," she replied.

The sheriff patiently listened while Tammy repeated her conversation with Toby Brown.

"Yeah, that was pretty stupid," he agreed when she finished speaking.

"What am I going to do?"

"You are going home and staying there like you should have done in the first place. I just finished speaking with Wilmont Sawyer, and he seemed genuinely surprised when I told him what had happened to Clara."

"I'm going to be staying at the cabin tonight and not at my own place in case my aunt tries to call on the landline. Zeke is coming over for supper, and I may ask him to spend the night in case whoever took my aunt returns thinking no one is at the house," Tammy said.

"Good idea. Zeke is not on the schedule tonight or tomorrow. Let me know immediately if you hear from Clara. Go home," the sheriff said sternly.

"I will, right after I stop at the Brown Bear Café to pick up some supper for myself and Zeke. I promise."

"Good. Now I have to go in and speak to Toby Brown before I go home for the night."

"He's been watching us out the window the whole time," Tammy said.

"I know. I saw him there when I walked up to your car."

Tammy pulled into the parking lot at the restaurant as her cell quacked, signaling a text message. It was from Zeke saying he was at her house, and she wasn't. She told him to stay put. She would be there shortly with supper and asked if he would mind spending the night at her aunt's cabin in case someone returned. He messaged back, saying he would, and he was going to run home for a set of clothes, let the dog out, and would be back before she returned.

She entered the café and was inundated with questions about her aunt, none of which she could really answer. Finally reaching the counter, she requested the fried shrimp and fish and chips off the special board. Tammy figured they could share the dinners and enjoy a mini seafood platter. Extra lemon slices, cocktail sauce, orders of coleslaw, and onion rings were added to the order.

Knowing she had beer and wine at home to drink, she passed on the milkshakes they usually got when eating at the café. Waiting for her order to go, Mrs. Cotton walked up and sat on the stool next to her.

"I want to apologize for my behavior at the grocery store," she said. "It is rude to gossip, and I know that, but us old ladies around here are so excited Zeke has finally broken down the wall he built around himself after Emily left him the way she did."

"It's okay. I know how small-town gossip works. I used to live here, remember?"

"It was still rude of me."

"I forgive you, and just so you know and hear it directly from me, Zeke and I are just friends. I don't even know if I'll be staying at the end of the summer. Aunt Clara may be closing Idle Chat, and I won't have much reason to stay."

"Personally, I think Zeke Peters would be enough of a reason to stay," Mrs. Cotton commented. "But, then again, I don't know how young people think nowadays."

"Not to change the subject, but have you been approached by anyone to sell your house and property?" Tammy asked.

"I sure have," the elderly woman answered, slamming her fist on the counter. "And I have told them all I'm not going anywhere. My husband built my house for me as a wedding present, and the only way I'll leave it will be through the front door on a gurney."

"Has anyone threatened you since you turned down their offers?"

"No, but weird things have been happening around my property."

"What do you mean? What weird things?"

"My car had flat tires three nights in a row. My phone lines had been cut, and I think someone was in my house while I was out. My cat, Felix, was wandering around in the back yard when I got home."

"Doesn't Felix go out?"

"My baby is an indoor cat because of all the coyotes in the area. He never goes out and has never even tried to go out an open door. When I pulled in the driveway, he ran up to the car, meowing loudly. He was not happy he was outside."

"Was anything amiss in the house?"

"Not that I could see. But next door, at the Grady property, they were emptying the house for demolition. I could see that darn Toby Brown standing on the front porch, glaring at me. There were other men there with him I didn't know, and I thought I knew everyone in this part of town."

"Is it Mr. Brown who is trying to buy your house?"

"It is, and Wilmont Sawyer. They are both low-life snakes and don't care a lick for anyone in this town but themselves."

"You be really careful, you hear me? We don't know who it was who took my aunt, and I would hate for you to be their next victim," Tammy said, cautioning her.

"I realized that today when I heard about what happened to Clara. I called my sister, and she is coming to stay with me for a few weeks, so I won't be at the house alone."

"Good idea, but you still need to be on your toes."

"Mabel is arriving tomorrow. I should be fine until then."

"I'm going to give you my cell phone number. If you have any problems at all, call me," Tammy said, pulling a pen and paper out of her purse.

"You and Zeke are made for each other. He did the same thing yesterday," Mrs. Cotton said, taking the paper.

"You're all set, Tammy," the waitress said, setting two brown bags in front of her on the counter. "Say hi to Zeke for me."

"Zeke, huh?" Mrs. Cotton said with a twinkle in her eye. "Have a nice supper with your *friend*."

Zeke's truck and the sheriff's cruiser were in the driveway when Tammy arrived at the cabin. They were sitting in the rocking chairs, deep in discussion, their faces showing the tension of their words.

"Hello, Sheriff," Tammy said, setting the bags on the steps. "Do you have news on my aunt?"

"None yet. The people who live at the end of the road did see a white pick-up truck leaving the area around the time of Clara's disappearance, but they didn't pay much attention to it, nor did they see who was driving it."

"This is nuts. How does someone just disappear into thin air?"

"Unfortunately, with the number of woods around here and the many hunting cabins that are only used a couple of months a year, there are many places to hide someone. It's just one of the possibilities where Clara could be," the sheriff replied.

"The sheriff was telling me he spoke to Toby Brown and got nowhere with him," Zeke said.

"He did admit he has a silent partner, but the person wanted to remain anonymous. Toby informed me if I wanted any more information, I could come back with a proper search warrant. As of right now, I don't have enough evidence against him to get a judge to sign one," Sheriff Becker said. "Then he opened the door for me to leave."

"So, the question is, why is he hiding behind a search warrant?" Zeke asked. "And who is the partner he is hiding?"

"I never trusted him again after he got caught embezzling funds from the local church. He swore he spent all the money and had none to return, but shortly afterwards, he bought the bowling alley."

"Did he get charged?"

"No. The minister was good friends with his parents, and they worked out a plan to repay the missing money, so Toby was never held accountable for anything he did. But his reputation was so badly damaged no one would utilize the bowling alley. I don't know how it's stayed open all these years," Zeke said.

"Maybe his silent partner has bailed him out," Tammy offered.

"Could be, but my question would be, why put more money into a failing business?" Zeke replied. "That wouldn't make much sense."

"Sheriff, just so you know, I talked to Mrs. Cotton earlier today, and she thinks someone broke into her house while she was out. She also told me Toby Brown was standing on the porch next door watching her. They are emptying the old Grady house for demolition. It seems they are advancing with their plans even though people are refusing to sell to them," Tammy stated.

"I don't like this. Clara is missing, and now they are watching Mrs. Cotton," Zeke said.

"Her sister is coming to stay with her, so she won't be alone. She arrives tomorrow," Tammy said. "I gave her my cell number in case she needed to call me."

"I did the same thing," Zeke said. "Great minds, I guess."

"I'm heading out," the sheriff said, standing up. "On my way home, I'll stop and check on Mrs. Cotton and make sure she is secure in her house for the night. Call me immediately if you hear from Clara."

"I will," Tammy promised.

"It's a gorgeous night. Why don't we eat out here on the porch?" Zeke suggested.

"I'll keep the front door open so we can hear the landline in case it rings. Do you want a beer or glass of wine with supper?"

"A nice cold beer sounds great," he answered, setting the bags of food up on the picnic table at the far end of the farmer's porch.

"Fish and chips and fried shrimp, nice choice," Zeke commented as Tammy returned with their beers.

"I figured we could divvy them up and have some of each," she said, sitting down.

They had just started to eat when the landline rang. Tammy ran for the phone.

"Hello!"

"Tammy," a voice whispered. "Help me."

"Aunt Clara, where are you?" Tammy yelled into the phone.

She could hear a scuffle on the other end of the line, and it went dead.

Zeke heard Tammy yelling into the phone and called the sheriff on his own cell phone.

"Oh, Zeke. My aunt got caught using the phone. I could hear them roughing her up to get it away from her. She didn't have time to tell me where she was," Tammy said, visibly upset.

"The good thing is we know she is still alive," he replied. "I don't think they'll do anything to her until she signs over the ceramic shop. We both know she'll never give in to them and sign her place away, which may play to her advantage."

"She is feisty, but I don't know if it's necessarily a good thing when dealing with people like this," Tammy said.

When the sheriff arrived, she repeated everything said during the phone call, which wasn't much. He asked Tammy if she heard anything in the background of the call that could signal where Clara was being held, and she hadn't. She watched him shake his head as he closed his notebook, and then she reinforced her promise to stay near the phone in case Clara made another attempt to call.

Not having much of an appetite left, she picked at her food and nursed her beer as Zeke ate. After finishing, they moved inside for the evening to escape the mosquitoes. Seeing she was still upset, he gave her a hug and told her everything would be okay. In that moment of tenderness shared between them, Tammy felt safe and secure. She wanted to believe him; she really did.

While Zeke watched a movie, Tammy pulled out her computer and a notebook. She started to search for any information she could find on Wilmont Sawyer, Toby Brown, and Flashpoint Realty. At two in the morning, she decided to call it quits as her eyes were tired from staring at the screen. Zeke had fallen asleep in the recliner while watching TV. She had him move to the spare room so he would be more comfortable for the remainder of the night. Tammy laid down on the couch, snuggled under a quilt her aunt had made, and placed both phones next to her head on the pillow before dozing off.

Chapter Six

Zeke was up early as he had an eight o'clock dentist appointment and left the cabin by seven-thirty. There was no coffee at her aunt's cabin, so Tammy locked up and headed to her own place for coffee, a shower, and clean clothes. The bird feeders needed to be filled as she had ignored them the past couple of days, and they were all but empty.

No one had been at Idle Chat to check on the business since the murder. Tammy finished her second cup of coffee and drove to the ceramic shop, telling herself she wouldn't be gone long and would return to wait for any more phone calls like she had promised the sheriff she would do.

The yellow police tape was still wrapped around the back of the building but was hanging willy-nilly from the wind. As she stared at the peacock key she had taken out to unlock the door, she realized Goodwin Scott's keys had never been found at either crime site, here at the shop, or where the truck was dumped.

It hit her in the moment whoever killed the delivery man still had a key to get into the ceramic shop, and she needed to change all the locks as soon as possible. She pulled out her cell phone, did a search, and found the closest locksmith, and called the number. The locksmith knew her aunt and was aware of all that had happened. He promised to meet Tammy at the shop at noon.

Entering the shop, she checked the register area first, making sure no one had been in the shop and messed with the register. Tammy opened the drawer underneath, and the deposit bag was still there containing the start-up cash for each day. Not wanting to tempt fate, she folded the bag in half and stuck it in her purse.

The desk sitting in the back of the area was a mess, like someone had rifled through what was there looking for something. Straightening things out, she noticed the checkbook for the business, the deposit ledger, and the two charge cards her aunt used to buy supplies were missing. And not thinking about fingerprints, she touched many of the items left behind.

What an idiot. I write mysteries, and the first thing I do is touch everything in question at a crime scene. Where is my brain?

She made two calls. One to the sheriff and one to her aunt's bank to put a freeze on the business account. As much as the bank president wanted to help her, Tammy was not on the account, and the bank could not do what she had requested. Instead, she asked if they could flag the account to see if anyone tried to gain access to it. He stated because Clara was a good friend of his he would flag the account as asked.

While waiting for the sheriff to arrive, Tammy continued to walk through the shop. She hadn't been back to clean up the area where the murder took place. The blood had been absorbed into the cement floor and turned a dark brown in color. There was a perfect trail of blood drops from the dock where Goodwin had been hit to where he had been carried to the kiln room and stuffed in the kiln. She stood there, fixated on the blood, trying to picture Goodwin's last few moments alive.

"Tammy! Are you here?"

"Back here, in the kiln room," she answered.

The sheriff joined her. She told him about the missing items off the desk and how she had realized the murderer still had a key to the ceramic shop and anywhere else in town where Goodwin delivered supplies.

"We've called all the people who Goodwin delivered to and warned them to change their locks. I guess we never thought about this place as it hasn't been open," the sheriff admitted. "What were you so deep in thought about when we walked into the room?"

"I was following the blood trail. It doesn't look like the body was dragged from the loading dock to here. Goodwin wasn't small, so whoever killed him had to be a good-sized person to carry him from there to here and to be able to hoist him into the kiln."

"Not ignoring your deductions, but have you noticed anything else missing?" the sheriff asked.

Before she could answer, Zeke walked into the kiln room and joined them.

"Nothing else, only the items I mentioned before. Oh, and I do need to tell you I rummaged through the stuff on the top of the desk when looking to see what was missing. I didn't even think about fingerprints," Tammy admitted, waiting for the sheriff to blow up.

Zeke eyed the sheriff, thinking the same thing was going to happen, but it didn't.

"You need to get the locks changed," he said instead.

"The locksmith is coming at noon to change them," Tammy said. "I know you said I need to stay at Aunt Clara's cabin, but I'm glad I came by to check on the shop, or I wouldn't have known someone had been in here."

"I'm going to the bank and talk to the manager," Sheriff Becker said.

"I already called them, and they have flagged the account for any activity," Tammy replied. "If we are done here, I need to go home to check the message machine to see if my aunt called again."

"Good observation on the build of the murderer, but we already figured that out. Please be careful and stay out of our investigation. Call me if you hear from Clara," the sheriff said, turning and walking out the door.

"I guess he doesn't want any of my help," Tammy said in a huff.

"He's only trying to keep you safe. He doesn't want the same thing to happen to you that happened to your aunt. You need to listen to him. I don't want anything to happen to you either."

"Thanks, I appreciate that," she said, smiling.

"The sheriff may appear gruff and unappreciative, but he is really a big old teddy bear. He has the overwhelming responsibility of protecting everyone in this town, even the ones who don't deserve it. It's not a job he takes lightly and Clara's disappearance is weighing heavy on him," Zeke said.

The couple reached the door to see the sheriff had already left. Tammy locked the door even though it really didn't do any good.

"I was on the computer last night researching Flashpoint Realty. Whoever

KILNED AT THE CERAMIC SHOP

the silent partner is, he doesn't want to be known as the name doesn't appear on any public records. The business was established two years ago, but Brown ran it out of the bowling alley before the mall office was acquired."

"It still baffles me as to where he came up with all the money to be buying up properties like he has been doing. I know he didn't get it from his parents as they're still not speaking to one another," Zeke stated. "He never paid them back a red cent after they bailed him out of trouble with the church. They have basically disowned him."

"So, who we need to be looking for is a person who is well off and can afford to sink money into a losing business and speculative projects. Do you know anyone who fits that bill?"

"I can think of a few, but the first name that pops into my mind is Wilmont Sawyer. He has more money than anyone else in this county. The big question would be why would he help a business he is in direct competition with for the same properties?"

"Unless he is using Flashpoint as a front because he knows the people around here don't like or trust him. He's counting on the fact they might sell to someone else to get back at him, but they are really selling to him and don't know it. Does that make any sense?"

"Yes, it does, in a roundabout way," he agreed. "But how do you prove it, and does it link him to Goodwin's murder?"

"I don't know yet. I haven't got that far," Tammy said. "Am I going to see you for supper?"

"I have my bowling league tonight."

"At Brown's alley?"

"No, we go over to Culver and bowl there. Most of the league is made up of local police and firemen, and none of us will step foot in Brown's place. Plus, there is a bar there, and we all sit around swapping stories after we're done bowling."

"I guess this is the universe's way of telling me I need to plant my butt on the couch and get some writing done," Tammy laughed. "If you get out early enough, I'll be at the cabin glued to my laptop."

"I usually don't get back from Culver until after midnight, so I doubt I'll be over."

"One more question before you go. Have the police checked out the properties Sawyer owns in their search for my aunt?"

"Yes, we have."

"Darn, I was hoping he might not be smart and keep her somewhere close by."

"Don't fool yourself. Wilmont Sawyer is a very smart man. He wouldn't make a stupid mistake like keeping Clara at one of his own properties."

"It was just a thought," Tammy said, sighing and getting into her car. "I'll see you tomorrow."

The answering machine was empty when she got back to the cabin. At her aunt's age, she clung to the older ways of technology. It made Tammy feel a little better knowing if she wasn't there, her aunt if afforded the time, could leave a message on the recorder. She had an hour before she had to be back at the shop, so she dragged out her laptop and opened it to the file she had started for her new book. Forty-five minutes later, she was still staring at the same page and hadn't added a single word to the manuscript.

"Aunt Clara where are you?" she asked, looking at a picture of her aunt sitting on the side table next to her. "Real life is so different from writing in an imaginary world. If this was a book, I would have solved your kidnapping already."

She closed her laptop. Right then and there, she vowed she would find her aunt and bring her home. Tammy left for the ceramic shop to meet the locksmith.

Jason Crumb was waiting for her when she arrived at Idle Chat. He had already walked around the building and made notes of how many new locks he would need and was ready to get to work. Four locks in all would need to be replaced: three on doors leading to the outside and one on the door between the loading dock and the rest of the interior building.

"I have been extremely busy this week," he said while working on the first lock. "I think Goodwin delivered to almost every business in town, and when his keys disappeared, everyone panicked and wanted their locks changed right away. Everyone that is except you and the bowling alley."

"We haven't been open since the day of the murder, and this morning was the first time I had been back since my aunt disappeared. Someone used those stolen keys and let themselves in while no one was around."

"So, I heard, and I am truly sorry. Clara is a wonderful person with a huge heart. I listen to the talk around town, and everyone is betting it is Wilmont Sawyer who has her stashed somewhere. Clara was the first person to stand up to him, and I hope she doesn't pay dearly for her actions."

Tammy felt like she was going to throw up. It was her who had talked her aunt into doing exactly what the locksmith had just mentioned. How could she live with herself if Clara never made it home again? Maybe she should have kept her opinions to herself and let her aunt sell the property when she first said she wanted to. She could have retired, Tammy could have returned to New York City, and all would be well. Except for the fact she wouldn't have been able to reconnect with Zeke.

"Miss. Excuse me?"

"I'm sorry. My thoughts were elsewhere."

"Can you unlock the loading dock door for me, please?"

"Sure, right this way," she said, leading him to the back of the shop.

"Is that blood?" he asked, stepping over it and not on it.

"Yes, it is. I'm sorry I haven't had time to clean up the shop yet. Did you say earlier the bowling alley hadn't requested their locks be changed yet?"

"That's right. I called to ask them about having the work done as they were on the list the sheriff had given me. At first, Mr. Brown refused, saying there was no need, but he called back a few hours later, saying maybe he should have it done just to be on the safe side."

"Interesting," Tammy mumbled. "I'm going to run across the street and get a coffee and bagel for lunch. Would you like something?"

"I would love a coffee, regular, please. I didn't have time this morning to get one before I started work. Thank you."

"I'll be right back."

Tammy placed her order at one counter and then moved to the second counter, where the register was located, to pay and wait for her items. The smells of fresh baked pastries and muffins reminded her of the café she used to stop at every morning on her way to work in the city. The woman behind the register kept staring at her and finally spoke.

"You're Clara's niece. I called the police on you when you were sitting in your car watching her shop."

"Yes, that would be me. I was the stalker," Tammy said, smiling. "I want to thank you for being so protective of my aunt and watching out for her."

"We all watch out for each other around here. I've been keeping an eye on her shop since it's been closed."

"Have you seen any vehicles pull into the parking lot in the last few days?"

"No, can't say I have. It's been quiet over there, but you might ask Mrs. Cotton if she's seen anyone. Her house is adjacent to the rear of the shop, and she would have a better view of any comings and goings."

"I will, thank you," Tammy said, thinking she wanted to check on the elderly woman anyway and see if her sister had arrived to stay with her.

Throwing a couple of dollars in the tip jar, she picked up her bagel and the two large coffees and left the café. As she waited to cross the street, she saw Toby Brown turn down the street and fly by the ceramic shop. He hadn't seen her, or if he did, he didn't let on he had. She gave the locksmith his coffee and set hers on the counter. He still had one more door to change over, so Tammy decided this was as good a time as any to go check on Mrs. Cotton. And, at the same time she might just see where Brown had gone.

"While you finish up, I'm going to go visit with Mrs. Cotton the next house over and make sure she is doing okay," Tammy said. "I should be back before you finish so I can pay you for your services."

"I'll be here. Say hi to her for me. Hattie Cotton is my grandma."

"I didn't know that. She is one spitfire of a lady," Tammy replied.

"Yes, she is. That's why she and Clara are such great friends. They are cut from the same cloth as people might say."

"She told me yesterday that her sister, Mabel, is coming to stay with her for a couple of weeks."

"That's great news. We don't like her living in the house by herself, but she refuses to leave it because of my grandpa, and he passed nearly twenty years ago."

"That's what she told me."

"If you think my grandma is a handful, wait until you meet Mabel. No one in the family messes with her, and whatever you do, don't ever tell her she is wrong. My dad made that mistake only once, and the rest of the family learned from his smackdown to bite their tongue when arguing with her," Jason chuckled. "She doesn't back down from anyone and will get right in your face to prove her point."

"I'll remember that. Thanks for the warning."

The closer Tammy got to the Cotton house, the louder an argument became which was emanating from the Grady house next door. Toby Brown was on the front porch arguing with an elderly woman Tammy had never seen before. Brown raised his fist in the air, and Tammy, afraid that he was going to strike the woman, broke into a dead run to get to the porch.

"What's going on?" Tammy demanded to know.

"You! Get off my property and take this crazy old bat with you!" Brown screamed.

"Mind your manners if your mother even taught you any in the first place. I'm not crazy. I know it was you who was in my sister's house while we ran to the grocery store. Felix was outside in the backyard again, and when we left, he was in the house. I don't know how you are getting in, but I will figure it out."

"Are you saying it wasn't you who broke into the house?" Tammy asked Brown, staring at his swollen eyes. "Mr. Brown, are you allergic to cats by any chance?"

"NO!"

"I find it very suspicious your eyes are watering and swollen. Both times the Cotton house has been broken into Felix was thrown outside. It's almost like the person didn't want the cat near them while they were in there."

"I have pine allergies," he stammered. "Not that it's any of your business."

"I'm warning you. Stay away from my sister and stay away from her house. She is not going to sell to you and never will. If I need to stay here until we both die and her grandson inherits the house, that's what I'll do."

"Come on, Mabel. We need to call the sheriff and let him question Mr.

Brown," Tammy said, gently taking the woman's arm to guide her down the steps.

A loud crash sounded inside the house.

"Is someone else here with you?" Tammy inquired.

"If you must know, Miss Nosy, there is a person inside appraising the larger pieces of furniture left behind by the Grady family. Now, both of you, beat it, and don't show your faces over here again."

"Or what?" Mabel asked, firming her stance and putting her hands on her hips. "You don't scare me, Mr. Brown. You just keep yourself and your empty threats away from Hattie's house. Heed your own advice."

Walking away, Tammy noticed there was no other car parked at the Grady house. If there was an appraiser inside, how did he get there? She was trying to envision Brown's car as it turned down the road when she was waiting to cross the street. There was no one else in the car with him.

"Mabel, are you okay?" Hattie asked as the two women came through the front door. "I told you not to go over there. He's dangerous. I thought he was going to strike you at one point."

"So did I," Tammy admitted. "Please don't confront him by yourself again, Mabel."

"Oh, pish! I brought my Thumper with me. That nasty, ill-mannered man doesn't stand a chance if he returns here."

"Thumper?"

"Yes, my Thumper," Mabel said, walking into the kitchen and returning with an aluminum baseball bat.

"That's all well and good, Mabel, but Toby Brown is twice your size, and if you don't get the first hit in quickly and right on target, I don't think the Thumper will help," Tammy said. "He may turn around and use it on you."

"It's never failed me before," she insisted.

"Just the same; I'm going to call the sheriff and tell him my suspicions about it being Toby Brown who is breaking into your house. I'm also going to ask he send a cruiser by the house occasionally just to check up on the both of you."

"That sounds good to me," Hattie said.

"Now, I have to get back to the shop. Someone named Jason Crumb is at Idle Chat changing all the locks. He's a really nice person," Tammy said, smiling.

"My grandson," Hattie exclaimed proudly. "He's such a good boy and quite a hard worker. I am leaving this house to Jason in my will when the time comes. He loved his grandpa."

"I keep telling her Jason already has a house," Mabel stated.

"I know, but it's much smaller than this one, and someday he may have a family of his own and need a larger place. If he doesn't want it, then he can sell it and start college funds for his children's futures," Hattie insisted.

"That makes sense," Mabel commented.

"Stay safe, ladies," Tammy said, escaping out the door before another conversation could begin.

My aunt's generation sure has some feisty ladies. One with a frying pan, one with a bat. They don't seem to back down from anything.

Jason was sitting in the back of his van when Tammy got back. He smiled, reached behind him, and produced a written invoice, handing it to her. She looked it over and asked him to come into the shop so she could get her wallet.

"All the shop's business accounts are frozen, so I'm going to pay this with my personal credit card," she said. "I hope that's okay."

"As long as the bill gets paid, it's fine by me," he said, running the card through his portable reader. "How did you like Mabel?"

"She's everything you warned me about and more. When I got there, she was fighting with Toby Brown and was right in his face like you said she would do," Tammy said.

"I don't like him. I don't trust him. When I finished changing his locks, he wanted to pay me at the end of the month. Said he didn't have any money. I insisted he pay me right then because I have been burned too many times."

"So, what happened?"

"He disappeared into the back office, and I heard him arguing with another guy. Next thing I know, he returns with a fistful of cash and pays the entire bill."

"Did you get a chance to see who he was arguing with?"

"No. Whoever it was stayed behind closed doors the whole time I was there. I didn't even know anyone else was in the building until I heard them yelling at each other."

"Thank you for all your work. I feel so much safer now that my aunt's shop is secured."

"All the locks match and use the same key. Here's a set of keys. I tested each one, and they work fine. If you need any more copies, just let me know."

"I will and thank you again."

"You are new to the area, well, not totally new, but you know what I mean. I want you to know Clara is on everyone's mind, and we are all hoping she returns home safe and sound," Jason said, walking to the door. "Bingo is not the same without her there on Sunday nights."

Tammy watched him leave and then checked each door to make sure the place was locked up tight. Sitting in her car, she called the sheriff and told him what had happened between Toby Brown and Mabel and her own observations of his swollen eyes and the cat being ejected from the house during each break-in.

Deciding on an early supper, she stopped at the Brown Bear Café and picked up a Reuben and fries. The next stop was at Braddock Wine and Liquors for a six-pack of beer and several different bottles of wine.

Tammy planned on staying at her aunt's cabin the rest of the afternoon and night. She would try to get some writing done, try being the keyword. There were no messages left on the answering machine. She ate her supper and then took a cup of hot tea out onto the porch to call her agent and let him know what was happening with her aunt.

He said he now understood why he hadn't received any pages and only the synopsis from her. He warned her to be extra careful and to check in periodically to let him know what was going on and if she was okay. She promised to do so and hung up.

Her aunt's neighbors drove by the cabin and waved as they passed. Other than that, all was quiet except for the emerging chirping of the crickets.

Tammy watched the sky's colors change over the tree line as she sipped her tea. Bright blues faded into streaks of oranges, purples, and pinks, and then to a dark grey. It was beautiful to watch but would have been so much more enjoyable if her aunt had been there sharing the sunset with her.

Finishing the last drop of tea, which was now cold, she stood up and went into the cabin. For the first time, she truly understood why her aunt loved it here in Braddock.

Chapter Seven

The next morning, Tammy hurried to her own cottage to complete her usual morning routine. She started a pot of coffee and went to feed the birds. Sitting on the steps, watching the birds frolic, she compiled all the information in her head that she already knew about her aunt's disappearance.

What if Wilmont Sawyer was the silent partner so he could purposely deceive the people of Braddock? He had plenty of money to back Brown at Flashpoint Realty, and he benefited from the partnership. But the bowling alley, that was something different. Why would a smart businessman pour money into a losing venture? Maybe Sawyer offered to bail the failing business out if Brown let him use his name for the bogus realty office. There were too many unanswered questions about who the silent partner was and why he wanted to remain anonymous. It was time for Tammy to return to Sawyer Realty and get some answers.

Checking the answering machine at her aunt's cabin before she left, the light was flashing red, which signaled a message had been left while she was gone. She ran to the machine and hit the play button. There were no words spoken directly in the recording, but Tammy could hear muffled voices in the background. It sounded like two men arguing, and then the line went dead. Unfortunately, she had no way of knowing if the message had been from her aunt or not.

Leaving the message as it was and not erasing it so she could play it for the sheriff, she locked the cabin and drove into town. This time, when she pulled up to Sawyer Realty, there was no sheriff's cruiser outside to deter

KILNED AT THE CERAMIC SHOP

her from going into the office.

The receptionist looked up and smiled as Tammy entered the office.

"May I help you?" she asked.

"I'd like to speak to Wilmont Sawyer, please."

"Have a seat, and I will see if he's available," she replied, pointing to a row of chairs near the front picture window.

Tammy perused the reception space. Various framed awards hung on the walls that had been placed there to impress anyone who walked into the office for the first time. Another wall displayed Sawyer family photos. The largest photo showed Wilmont, his wife, and their six kids. Judging from the appearance of Wilmont, the picture must have been taken quite a few years ago. She looked around for a more recent picture, but there was none.

"Can I help you?" a voice asked from behind her.

She turned, and the smile instantly left Wilmont's face.

"What do you want?" he snarled.

"I need to talk to you about my aunt's disappearance," she stated.

"I'll tell you the same thing I told the sheriff. I had nothing to do with Clara going missing, and if I knew anything, anything at all, I would be the first one to step up and say something to clear my good name."

"Good name? Seriously? You bully old ladies to get them to sell to you, among the other sketchy business dealings you have been tied to. You broke my aunt's car window and smiled when you did it. Your good name was tarnished long ago."

"I may get pushy, raise my voice, and sometimes utter a threat now and then, but I would never cross the line and stoop to kidnapping someone. I have to live in this town, too."

"Do you know Toby Brown?"

"Yes. I sold the bowling alley to his parents, who later turned it over to him. They thought it would keep him out of trouble if he became a responsible business owner, but the joke was on them."

"What do you mean?"

"He's been in more trouble since he owned the place. He sold drinks to minors and lost his liquor license, so the bar was shut down. At one point, the police thought he was selling stolen car parts out of the back of the bowling alley, but it was never proved."

"So, are you saying he is not to be trusted?"

"He's a snake. No one wants anything to do with him. I can't believe the bowling alley is still open or he had the money to open a real-estate business."

"I have been told he has a silent partner at Flashpoint Realty. Is that partner you?" Tammy asked directly.

The receptionist spit out her coffee.

"I am so sorry," she said, reaching for some tissues on her desk.

Tammy stared at the receptionist, waiting for an explanation.

"Toby Brown is Sally's brother. Many years ago, he convinced us both to invest large sums of money in a vineyard he wanted to buy and operate. He assured us we would double our original investments within a year of the first harvest."

"And?"

"We gave him the money, and he bought the vineyard. He put a minimal down payment on the place and never made another mortgage payment after that. The bank foreclosed, and we lost everything. To this day, I believe he pocketed all the money we gave him. Wilmont filed a lawsuit against him on behalf of both of us, trying to recoup some of our investment, but there wasn't enough evidence, and the lawsuit went nowhere. Toby owes both of us so much money Wilmont would never ever go into business with him again," Sally said. "Like my boss said, my brother can't be trusted."

"He has no conscience and had the nerve to move back to town. That's when he stole the money from the church, and his parents bailed him out again," Wilmont said.

"So, you have no idea who his silent partner could be?"

"No. I can't believe anyone in this town would even think about becoming his partner unless they were looking to end up in jail," Sally replied.

"And you swear you had nothing to do with my aunt's disappearance," Tammy asked, staring Wilmont Sawyer right in the eye.

"I like Clara. She is the first person who has ever stood up to me, and I admire her for that. I would never hurt her. That doesn't mean I won't still go after her property."

"I guess I'm done for now, but I may be back if I have any further questions. Nice looking family, by the way," she said as she exited the front door.

On the drive home, Tammy replayed the conversation in her mind she just had with Wilmont. He seemed to be telling the truth, but, like the sheriff said, you couldn't tell if he was being honest or just a great actor. She would still keep an eye on him regardless of her gut feeling he was telling the truth.

Words easily flowed the whole afternoon. Tammy stayed in the cabin waiting for that all-important call from her aunt. Five hours had flown by as she finished an outline for her own use and chapters three and four of her new mystery. She had only stopped to look at the clock because her stomach had growled, and it was starting to get dark outside. Closing the laptop after accomplishing a good day of writing, Tammy ran to her own place to move her coffee maker and a suitcase of clothes to her aunt's so she wouldn't have to keep running between the two residences.

Clearing a spot off the counter next to the sink, she set up her coffee maker. After preheating the oven, Tammy slid a frozen pizza on the middle rack and set the timer on top of the stove. Reaching into the cabinet above her coffee maker to get a glass for her wine, she selected the biggest one she could find and set it on the counter.

Swinging the cabinet door closed, Tammy was greeted by a face peering in the kitchen window at her. She let out a scream, and the man turned and fled. After the first few moments of being startled and dispersed, she flew out the back door to see if she could detect where the person had gone, but he was nowhere in sight. The sheriff was called again.

Tammy lit two citronella candles to keep the mosquitoes away and sat on the front porch waiting for the sheriff to arrive. To calm her nerves, she poured herself a large glass of wine and sat in the candlelit darkness. The timer went off in the house, signaling the pizza was done. She left it sitting on the top of the stove.

Sheriff Becker pulled into the driveway. He was in the car for several minutes talking on his radio before he approached the porch where Tammy was sitting. He sat down opposite her at the picnic table and let out a loud sigh.

"Bad day?" she inquired.

"You might say that. We can't catch a break in the case to find Clara. We were hoping the stolen credit cards from Idle Chat would be used, and we could trace who used them. But they were found in a dumpster behind the Spot-on Printing Shop, two doors down from Sawyer Realty. They were wiped clean, and not a single fingerprint was found on them, not even Clara's."

"What about the checkbook and the ledger?"

"The checkbook was there, and it had been shredded. We have someone attempting to reconstruct it, but I don't know if they'll be able to or not. The ledger was there, but all the pages had been ripped out of it."

"So, whoever originally took them didn't want to get caught with them in their possession and dumped everything," Tammy reasoned. "There had to be an entry in the checkbook or the ledger they didn't want to be seen."

"That's what we were thinking, hence the attempt at reconstructing the pages. What happened here today?"

Tammy told him about the man peering in the window. She believed it was the silent partner with the long black hair. After the initial shock wore off, she tried to follow him, but he had disappeared into the woods. Next, they listened to the curious message that had been left on the phone.

"Does your aunt have any extra tapes for the machine? I'd like to take this one to the lab and see if they can clean it up so we can hear what's being said," the sheriff requested.

"You can take it. There's a whole drawer of blanks in the desk."

The sheriff placed the miniature tape in his shirt pocket. Reiterating for her to be careful, he left. The pizza she had cooked was cold, hard as a cement block, and not at all appetizing. She dumped it in the trash barrel next to the stove.

As worried as she was about her aunt's well-being, she knew she had to buckle down and get more writing done. Tomorrow, she would spend the whole day at the cabin concentrating on her new novel. Grabbing an apple out of the fridge, she watched the early news and then went to bed.

Working on her second pot of coffee, the words flew out of her head and onto the computer screen. She was deep into writing a scene of a sister discovering the murder of her younger sibling when the images of Goodwin Scott stuffed in the kiln emerged in her brain. Remembering the punch in the gut feeling when she discovered it was someone her aunt was close to, she deleted the last ten pages she had just completed. They were stiff and unrealistic. Living through finding a dead body and seeing actual blood spatter had changed Tammy.

Zeke told her to use her new knowledge to improve her writing. She put herself in the sister's place and started to write again, drawing on her own real-life experience. An hour later, she was rereading the new pages and feeling much better about the sister's reactions. They were geared more toward human feelings, which made the scene tug at the reader's heart, even if it was found out later the sister really committed her sibling's murder.

Breaking for lunch, she sat on the porch in the sunshine, eating her turkey club and doing more research on Flashpoint Realty. No matter what site she brought up, there was no mention of a partner. To anyone else, it would appear Toby Brown was the sole owner, but Tammy knew different. She decided to stake out the bowling alley the next day and watch to see who went in and out.

The alarm was set on her phone, as she wanted to wrap up her writing by four-thirty. Zeke was coming over for supper, and she needed to start preparing what she was going to serve him. She boiled some red potatoes to make potato salad with mayo, mustard, chopped-up hard-boiled eggs, and pickles. Next, she husked some fresh corn on the cob that she had picked up at a local roadside stand on her way home the previous day. Two, inch-thick ribeye steaks were seasoned and ready to go on the grill.

This is eating fit for royalty.

The potato salad was in the fridge chilling, the corn was in the boiling water, and the steaks had been put on the grill. Tammy sat at the picnic table with a beer, keeping an eye on the steaks so they wouldn't burn.

At five forty-five, Zeke's truck pulled into the driveway. He was on his phone and not looking very happy. Exiting his truck, he slowly walked up to the porch and plunked down on the picnic table bench.

"You don't look very pleased. Have you found out something about my aunt?"

He didn't answer, and Tammy feared the worst.

"Zeke! Answer me."

"It has nothing to do with Clara. We still have no new leads."

"Then what is it?"

"Emily is back from California. That was her on the phone. She is staying at her mother's house and wants to see me," he said.

Tammy got up to turn the steaks. She kept quiet because she didn't know what to say. They weren't dating or even boyfriend and girlfriend, so she really had no right to say much of anything. They were just friends. Sitting back down, she waited for Zeke to speak.

"She said she made a huge mistake leaving me and wants me to give us another chance."

Tammy's first thought was she would be returning to New York after all. The only other reason she was contemplating staying in Braddock was now slipping away. She stared at Zeke, waiting for him to continue, but he sat there silently.

"What are you going to do?" she finally asked, getting up to take the steaks off the grill.

"I don't know. I never thought I would see her again."

"Do you still have feelings for her?"

"I'll probably always have some kind of feelings for her. We spent six years together. It's just she has caught me totally off guard, showing up out of nowhere like this."

"Are you going to see her?"

"We agreed to meet at The Brown Bear tomorrow for lunch."

"You have to do what you think is right," she said, trying to sound neutral. "Do you want a beer?"

"Seriously? You're not upset she's back?"

"I have no say in the matter. I haven't been back in Braddock long enough to pass any kind of opinion on your past history."

"I didn't ask you what you know. I asked you what you think."

"The truth?"

"Of course, I wouldn't expect anything else from you," he insisted.

"What I think? Okay. It bothers me that Emily can just show up and think you will pick up where you left off without even taking into consideration you might have moved on with someone else. And it bothers me even more there is nothing to say she wouldn't just up and leave again whenever she feels like it like she did last time. That's what I think. Are you happy?"

"Yes, I am," he said, moving to sit beside her on the bench.

"Why?"

"Because I know right now we are just friends, but sometime in the future, I was hoping for a more serious relationship with you. Truthfully, I agreed to meet Emily tomorrow to tell her I have met someone new and moved on without her."

"Really?"

"Yes, really," he said, smiling. "I think I could use a beer now."

"Grab the steaks, and let's go eat the awesome supper I have planned for us," Tammy said, opening the door to the cabin. "I can smell the fresh corn cooking from out here."

The food was set on the kitchen table, along with fresh bottles of beer. The couple dug in and were enjoying their meal when Zeke stopped eating and stared at Tammy.

"What? Have I got kernels stuck in my teeth?" she asked, setting down her corn.

"I have to ask you this. You said you were only going to be here for the summer to help out your aunt that day in the parking lot. Then, you said there would be no reason to stay if your aunt closed the ceramic shop on the day of Goodwin's murder. How do I know you won't pack up and go back to New York and leave me like Emily did?"

Tammy could see the hurt in his eyes as he asked his question. He had been burned by a relationship in the past, and she could tell he never wanted to go through anything like that again. The walls were starting to go up around him again, and he was backing away from her out of fear.

76

"I did say those things, didn't I?"

"Yes, you did."

"In my defense, both of those things were said before we started spending more time together."

"True, but that doesn't mean you aren't still thinking in the back of your mind about going back to the city."

"I'll let you in on a little secret. I am enjoying being back in Braddock and living a slower-paced lifestyle again. I'm enjoying my birds, wearing my jeans and sneakers instead of suits and high heels, and when I was shopping the other day for casual clothes, I kept telling myself I would go back and pick up the items I liked for the autumn and winter here in the cold state of Maine."

"So, you're not going back to the city?"

"I still plan on buying Idle Chat and letting my aunt run it like she always has. I'm pretty sure once whoever is causing all the problems is behind bars, things will settle down, and my aunt will go back to the shop," Tammy said, reaching for the butter. "In the short time I have been home, I realized what I left behind when I moved to the city. There will be times I have to leave for book tours, but I will always come back to Braddock."

"Good. I don't think I could go through another break-up like I did with Emily."

"I would never do something like that to you. If I wasn't sure about staying here, I would tell you so and stop the relationship in its tracks."

"Promise me, if anything ever changes, you will tell me right away so we can fix whatever it is that has gone wrong," Zeke requested.

"I promise. Now, take your beer and follow me. I want to show you what made me decide to stay here."

Tammy led Zeke out to the porch and pulled the two rocking chairs side by side, facing the sunset. They sat in silence as the sky did its dance, changing colors. The chirping of the crickets grew louder and louder as darkness fell.

"This is what made me want to stay here. I'm sure my aunt sits out here all the time watching the beautiful colors and drinking her wine," Tammy sighed. "Wasn't the sunset stunning?"

"Yes, it was, and I'm sure Clara will be back soon enough to enjoy the summer evenings on her porch."

"I hope you're right. Unfortunately, the mosquitoes arrive at night. Let's go inside before we get eaten alive," Tammy said, swatting at the bugs buzzing around her ears.

"Find something to watch on TV, and I'll grab us a couple more beers," Zeke suggested.

They had just got comfortable on the couch when a massive explosion went off behind the cabin, shaking it and everything inside it.

"What the…" Zeke said, making a run for the back door with Tammy close behind.

Chapter Eight

They stood frozen on the back porch of the cabin, watching blue-tinted flames shooting into the night sky. The cottage where Tammy had been living was totally engulfed, and there wasn't much left of it after the explosion. The fingers of the fire reached almost as high as the treetops.

"Call 911 and stay here," Zeke said, taking off in the direction of the fire.

Tammy made the call while watching Zeke circle the burning structure and then break into a run into the woods. She could hear the firetruck's sirens in the distance and knew they were on their way. The cottage was a total loss, and she knew the only thing they would be able to do would be to keep the fire from spreading into the woods and possibly to her aunt's cabin. Zeke returned from the darkness of the woods, and Tammy ran to join him in the yard. The heat forced them to back away from the burning structure.

"Why did you go into the woods?" Tammy yelled over the crackling of the fire.

"I saw someone crouching behind a tree, watching the place burn. I took off after him but lost him in the dark."

"You think the fire was set on purpose? I could have been in there this time of night."

"I think whoever did this was watching us and knew we were at Clara's place. I believe this was done as a warning and not meant to hurt anyone," Zeke replied.

"A warning? Not meant to hurt anyone? Aunt Clara is going to be heartbroken. She loved that little cottage. Wait until I get my hands on whoever did this."

"This doesn't make any sense. Why blow up a cottage when whoever it was who did this has no interest in this property, and Clara isn't even here to see the destruction?" Zeke asked.

"Maybe they made a video and are going to show it to my aunt. They might tell her she caused my death to get her to sign over the property. She has no way of knowing I was at her place and not in the cottage when the explosion took place," Tammy said.

"True. I just hope Clara stays strong and doesn't give in to them. If she signs the property over, she's as good as dead because she knows who they are."

The fire trucks came to a screeching stop in front of the fire. Men scrambled and got busy hooking up the hoses to the water truck, as there were no public hydrants close enough to Clara's property to use.

Locals started to appear to see what was happening but watched from the street and driveway so as not to get in the way. The sheriff joined Tammy and Zeke in the yard. They watched as the firemen skillfully corralled the fire to keep it away from the woods surrounding the back of the cottage. Within half an hour, they had the fire under control and almost out.

Tammy explained to the sheriff they were in Clara's cabin and heard the explosion but didn't actually see it when it happened. Zeke told the sheriff about the man in the woods and how he thought the fire was intentionally set. He explained his theory it was a warning and not meant to kill anyone.

"Are you okay, Tammy?' the sheriff asked.

"I'm ten times angrier than I am afraid. All my new clothes and apartment items I brought from New York have been destroyed. Not to mention Aunt Clara's cottage is gone, and for what? Nothing!"

"I think they just poked the bear, as they say," Zeke commented, glancing at Tammy.

"I think you're right," the sheriff agreed. "Do you feel safe enough to stay here by yourself tonight?"

"I'll be fine. Whoever did this wouldn't dare to return here tonight. Besides, my aunt has the whole cabin booby-trapped if anyone dares to come near it."

"Your aunt is a corker," the sheriff chuckled.

"Yes, she is. I just hope she stays strong wherever she is right now," Tammy said.

"Don't go near the cottage. The fire marshal is out of town but will be back in the morning. I want him to go over this place with a fine-tooth comb. If this was set, he will be able to tell us how, and it might give us a clue as to who has Clara."

"Sheriff, the fire is out, and there shouldn't be any flare-ups," the fire chief said, walking up to the group. "We checked for hot spots and didn't find any. I believe the cause was the propane tank. One whole side of it is blown completely away. Ed will be able to tell you more when he gets home tomorrow."

"Thank you, Chief, and please thank your crew, too," Tammy said. "I know my Aunt Clara would have appreciated all your hard work."

"Is there any word on Clara yet?"

"No, not yet. We are still working on it," the sheriff answered.

"Everyone around town is keeping their eyes and ears open. We'll find her. Don't you worry, Tammy, she'll come home safe and sound," the chief said.

"After this latest stunt, I'm really afraid for her. They appear to be getting more desperate," Tammy replied.

"Just keep thinking positive thoughts," the chief said. "Let's go, guys. Get those hoses rolled up."

The fire department left, and Tammy and Zeke walked the sheriff to his car.

"Make sure you keep all the exterior spotlights on around the perimeter of the yard throughout the night," the sheriff instructed. "If they do return, the lights may deter them from approaching the cabin."

"I have to go home and let Blinky out, but I can come back and spend the night," Zeke suggested.

"That might not be a bad idea," the sheriff agreed.

"I'll be fine. My aunt has a small guest room, and she already has the window boobytrapped. I'll set up some cans at the door."

"Stubborn, just like Clara," the sheriff stated.

"I'll take that as a compliment," Tammy said, smiling.

"I'm heading home for the night. If you need anything, call my cell phone," the sheriff said. "Zeke, I'll see you at work tomorrow."

"I'm going to finish my warm beer and head out, too," Zeke said.

Twenty minutes later, Tammy found herself alone in the cabin. It was eerily quiet after all the confusion earlier in the evening. Walking around from room to room, she double-checked the homemade alarm systems her aunt had put in place. She took her small overnight bag into the guest room to take an inventory of what clothes she had left. Including the clothes she was wearing, she had two pairs of jeans, three tee shirts, one sweater, and a few pairs of socks. Undergarments were in short supply as she only had one change she would use the next day. The only shoes she had were the one pair of sneakers which were on her feet.

"I guess after my stakeout at the bowling alley, I'll have to go back to the mall to do some more shopping," Tammy said, placing the only clothes she had on the extra bed in the room. "And just to be on the safe side, I'll make sure I take my computer with me when I leave the cabin."

She changed into her sweats and crawled into bed. Laying in the darkness of the room, the spotlights around the property made it look like daytime outside. Her first thoughts were of her aunt. Tammy hoped she hadn't been subjected to a video of the cottage burning and being told her niece was dead. After Goodwin's death, the current events and lies would break Clara for sure.

Her cell phone rang. It was Zeke checking in on her before he went to bed. Tammy could hear Blinky barking in the background. His owner explained he said the word bed, and the dog was impatient to go upstairs. They said goodnight, and Zeke promised to call her tomorrow before he went to work at three.

At sunrise, Tammy stood on the back porch of the cabin, sipping her coffee. The remains of the cottage looked even more dismal in the daylight. The only thing left standing in the burnt pile of rubble was the front section of the propane tank. Tammy could see one of her birdfeeders, half-burnt, swaying from its shepherd's hook at the front corner of the walkway. Her patio set had melted in the fire, and her new grill hadn't fared any better.

The other feeders she had hung in the trees at the edge of the yard were intact, and the birds were happily eating their morning breakfast. She watched them flit around, each one dodging the other one when approaching the small holes that released the seed. They were blissfully unaware of the previous night's activities.

The bushes containing the various nests along the front of the cottage were gone. She was sick inside thinking about the mother and baby birds who perished in the explosion. While she was out, she would have to pick up more bags of seed. Several new feeders were needed, and Tammy would place them far away from the burnt-out structure to give the birds a new start.

She was inside refilling her mug when someone knocked on the front door. Peeking through the peep hole, she saw the sheriff and another man she didn't know. She opened the door.

"Morning, Tammy. This is Ed Shaw. He's the fire marshal for our county. I wanted to introduce you in case you looked out a window and saw a strange man poking around," the sheriff said. "Knowing you, poor Ed would be chased off via a shovel."

"Nice to meet you, Mr. Shaw," Tammy said, ignoring the last comment made by the sheriff.

"Ed, please. One quick question. Have you had any problem with the appliances in the cottage?"

"No, none. Everything was working fine," she replied. "Can I tag along and watch? I might learn something."

"Tammy is a mystery writer."

"I know who she is. Clara insisted I buy her first book, and I have enjoyed each one ever since. Yes, you can come with us, but stay out of the way," Ed said.

They walked across the yard together, Tammy listening to every word Ed was speaking into his hand recorder. He went directly to the propane tank.

"The back of the tank is blown away, and if you look at the direction of the intensity of the fire, this side of the cottage sustained more damage than the far end of the structure," Ed explained, walking around the tank and taking notes. "This is where the explosion originated from."

Tammy began taking notes in a little notebook she carried around with her in case an idea for a new book hit her at a strange moment. All these tidbits of information could be used in one of her future books.

"Sheriff, look at this," Ed said, kneeling next to the part of the tank that was still intact.

On the ground was a badly burned section of a pipe. It was lying where the blown-away section of propane tank had originally been. The faint smell of gunpowder still hung in the air.

"I need to get my crew out here. This is part of a pipe bomb. It looks like it was attached to the bottom of the tank to blow it up. We need to scour the area for all the pieces of the bomb we can find."

"So, this was deliberately set?" Tammy asked.

"Uh, yeah, it was done on purpose. This was not a tank or valve malfunction. I need to tape off this entire area, and no one but my men will be allowed inside the tape."

"A bomb moves this up to a whole new level. Kidnapping wasn't bad enough for these people," the sheriff said.

"If you had been in the cottage, we wouldn't be speaking right now," Ed said to Tammy. "No one inside would have survived the blast."

"Maybe Zeke was right. This could have been done as a warning," the sheriff stated.

"It's one heck of a warning if it's all it was meant to be. Be extremely careful. As we walked out here, I noticed your aunt's cabin is also hooked up to a propane tank."

"It might be smart to stay at the bed and breakfast in town. I know you won't be near the phone, but your safety has to come first," the sheriff suggested.

"I'll think about it," she said.

"There's not much to think about," Ed said. "Clara would never put your life before hers or any material things she has in her cabin. That's not who your aunt is, and I'm sure deep down you know that, too. Family always comes first."

"My aunt's tank is set quite far away from the house in its own locked shed. The lines into the house are all underground."

"That's even worse," the sheriff said. "A padlock won't deter someone for very long, and it's close to the woods leading to the main road for an easy escape."

"I'm still going to stay here tonight. There is too much of a police presence for them to come back so quickly. I have a gut feeling I'll hear from my aunt tonight, and I have to be here," Tammy insisted.

"My men will arrive in about an hour, and they'll be here most of the day. I have to leave for Fulton as there was a factory fire over there last night, but I will check in with my team periodically," Ed said, walking away. "Sheriff, I'll call you with any information we get."

"Thanks, Ed."

"He seems really nice," Tammy said, watching him walk to his truck.

"Ed is brilliant in the field of fire science. He's been called out of state many a time to testify in court regarding arson cases. He is one of the tops in his field nationwide."

"Maybe he'll let me pick his brain when I need expert advice for a book," Tammy said.

"I'm sure he will. He loves to talk about his job, but not many people are interested in what he has to say. It's too bad, really, because he can spin quite a story."

"I'll have to have him over for dinner some night. After I find a new place to live, that is."

"I'd suggest going to a local realtor to find a short-term rental, but considering who you have to choose from in this area to work with, I'd stick to the newspaper or word of mouth."

"True. If need be, I can stay here until my aunt returns… if she returns," Tammy said hesitantly.

"We'll find Clara," the sheriff said, putting his arm around her shoulder. "Just stay positive, okay?"

"I'll try."

"Oh, geez, it's ten past ten. I was supposed to be at the town hall at ten for a budget meeting with the selectmen. Without Clara being there, I hope we can still have the meeting. I'll be in touch."

"Call me on my cell phone if you need to get in touch with me. I have to do some clothes shopping to replace what I lost in the fire. I'll be at the mall," Tammy yelled, not wanting to tell the sheriff a portion of the day she was going to be staking out the bowling alley.

He waved out the cruiser window in acknowledgment and drove away.

Tammy showered, dressed, and was ready to go half an hour later. She had gathered her computer, her purse and borrowed her aunt's camera because hers had been lost in the fire. They had identical cameras, as she had sent the same one she had to her aunt a few years ago for Christmas. Securing the cabin, Tammy left for her stakeout.

Driving past the bowling alley several times, she figured out the best place to park her car so she could see the side and rear entrance without being too conspicuous, which was at the business next door. She had her binoculars and the camera with the zoom lens sitting next to her on the front seat. Tammy settled in with her travel mug of coffee and the snacks she had brought with her from the cabin.

An hour passed with no activity. Tammy wondered if the place was even open and searched on her phone for the bowling alley and its hours of operation. The business opened at noon. It was ten to, and a car pulled into the parking lot behind the building she recognized as Toby Brown's car. He sat in his car for several minutes. When he finally climbed out, Tammy could see he was on the phone, and by the look on his face, he was not involved in a pleasant conversation. Walking up onto the loading dock platform, he unlocked the door and disappeared inside.

Now that Toby is here, maybe his silent partner will show himself.

She hadn't even finished her thought when another vehicle pulled in next to Toby's car. It looked to be a new car and of an expensive make. Tammy picked up her camera and focused the picture on the new arrival. An older woman, well-dressed and jewelry laden, exited the car. She locked it and set the alarm. Tammy took at least ten shots of the woman before she entered

86

the bowling alley through the side door.

Maybe Zeke will know who she is.

It wasn't very long before the woman returned to her car and left. Another hour passed with no other visitors, not even customers. Tammy decided to give it up for the day and go shopping. Maybe with Toby Brown in the bowling alley, she could see if someone else was manning the Flashpoint Realty office.

Arriving at the mall, Tammy parked in the back parking lot near the realty office. The blinds were closed to the outside, and when she went inside the mall entrance, the door leading into the office was locked.

"I am going to find out who you are," she said, shading her eyes from the mall lights and peering in the door.

A group of kids walked by, giving her a funny look when they heard her talking to herself. She stared directly at them. Laughing at the fear on their faces as they scurried to get away, she could only imagine they thought she was some kind of nutcase.

The next few hours were spent replacing all the clothes she had recently bought and lost in the fire. Tammy went from store to store, adding to the bags she was already carrying. When she was done, she had enough clothes she could wear for a full week's time before doing laundry. She also splurged on several pairs of shoes, two of which were different-colored sneakers than the ones she had on her feet.

Her phone rang in her back pocket. It was Zeke checking in as he promised before he left for work. He told her he was off the following day and planned on checking out the properties Wilmont Sawyer owned in town again. The sheriff might have thought the realtor was telling the truth, but Zeke wasn't so sure. If he was holding Clara, he might be moving her around. She agreed to go with him, and he said he would pick her up at ten.

On the way home, she stopped at The Brown Bear to pick up some supper. Mrs. Cotton and her sister were in a booth near the front door. While Tammy waited for her order to go, she joined the two women in their booth.

"And how is everyone doing tonight?" she asked.

"We had to get out of the house," Mabel complained.

"Why? Is everything all right?"

"That blasted Toby Brown will not leave my sister alone. He knocks on the door every day, at least twice a day, trying to get her to sell. He won't take no for an answer," Mabel replied.

"Did you call the sheriff to complain?" Tammy suggested.

"I did," Hattie said. "The sheriff told me he wasn't breaking any law by knocking on our door unless we had a restraining order taken out against him or unless he assaulted us. He said there was nothing he could do."

"Unfortunately, I believe that's true. What are you going to do about the situation?"

"Jason, my grandson, has been staying at the house with us. But he had to go out of town for a big job over in Fulton. I swear Brown is watching the house or has someone watching the house for him because not ten minutes after Jason was gone, Brown showed up knocking on the door. He didn't come near the place while Jason was there with us."

"Could someone be next door at the old Grady house, watching you from there?"

"I haven't seen anyone but Brown going in and out. Most times, he's removing a piece of furniture or something he has sold from the place," Mabel answered.

"I did overhear him one time when he was standing on my front porch talking on the phone. He was saying until they bought up a few more properties, they were going to hold off razing the Grady mansion because of the cost," Hattie said, putting sugar in her coffee for the second time. "Oh, dear, did I already put sugar in my coffee? That man has me so frazzled I can't think."

"Be careful when you get home. You don't know if he has been inside again, even though the sheriff did say something to him about it," Tammy warned. "You still have my phone number, right?"

"Yes, and we have Zeke's, too," Hattie said, patting the side of her purse. "Speaking of Zeke, how is your *friend* doing?"

"He's doing fine. Most of his time is taken up right now looking for my aunt."

"Still no word on Clara?" Hattie asked.

"Not yet," Tammy said. "We're going out tomorrow and look for her."

"I send a request up every night for her safe return," Hattie said. "This town has gone to heck in a handbasket."

"Hopefully, when we find out who is responsible for Goodwin Scott's death and my aunt's disappearance, things will calm down and return to normal. I came here expecting a quiet, boring summer, but this place has been anything but."

"Tammy, your order is ready," the waitress shouted.

"I have to go. Please be careful, and don't hesitate to call if you need anything," she said, getting up from the booth. "I'm only a couple of miles away."

Back home, Tammy had to make several trips from the car to the cabin to get all her purchases inside. After her new clothes were in the guest room, she returned to the car for her supper. As she was crawling into the front seat to retrieve the container of food, a cruiser pulled into the driveway next to her car. Looking grim as he approached her, Sheriff Becker held out a plastic evidence bag for her to see.

"Where did you get that?' Tammy demanded.

Chapter Nine

"Do you recognize it?" Zeke asked, joining the discussion.

"That's the contract I gave to my aunt to look over for the sale of the ceramic shop. Where did you get it? Have you found my aunt?"

"Two kids were messing around at the vacant drive-in, and they found it and a purple cardigan in one of the abandoned buildings."

"My aunt was wearing a purple sweater the day she disappeared. She wasn't there?"

"No. There was a cot, a blanket, and some empty food containers, but no sign of Clara," Zeke replied. "It looks like we might have just missed her. Some of the food was still fresh and couldn't have been there very long."

"Doesn't Wilmont Sawyer own that property?" she asked.

"Yes, he does," the sheriff said.

"And what better place to hide someone than somewhere that is deserted," Tammy mumbled.

"We are on our way over to Wilmont's office now. I wanted to verify this was the contract you gave to your aunt before we accused him of kidnapping Clara."

"I guess he is a good liar after all. Before you leave, I need you to look at a picture of someone to see if you know them or not."

She grabbed the camera out of the car and keyed up the pictures she took at the bowling alley.

"Do you know who this person is?" she asked, turning the camera screen in their direction. "I took this at the bowling alley this morning."

"That's Elizabeth Brown, Toby's mother," Zeke answered. "That's weird, as I thought he and his parents weren't speaking after the church episode."

"What were you doing at the bowling alley?" the sheriff asked.

"I thought I could take pictures of who went in and out to see if Toby Brown's silent partner would show up there. This woman, his mother, was the only one who visited him."

"I thought I told you to stay out of the investigation."

"I didn't go near the place. I stayed in the parking lot next door and parked behind some bushes so I wouldn't be seen. I guess it doesn't matter now that we know Sawyer has my aunt. Judging by her appearance, she has money. I wonder if she's bankrolling her son's business?"

"I highly doubt it," the sheriff replied. "Her husband would cut her off if he knew she was even visiting her son, never mind giving him any money. He must be out of town on one of his business trips."

"Thomas Brown made it really clear no one in the family should have anything to do with Toby, or they would lose their inheritance," Zeke added.

"Maybe she's helping him in secret," Tammy suggested.

"I don't think so. Elizabeth loves her money and takes great pleasure in flaunting her wealth around town. If I hadn't seen the picture for myself, I wouldn't have believed she would be taking a chance of aggravating her husband and losing everything she has," the sheriff said, glancing at the picture again. "Let's go, Zeke. We have to bring in Wilmont Sawyer for questioning."

"I'll let you know if we still need to look around tomorrow," Zeke said as he headed for the cruiser. "Hopefully, Sawyer will give up Clara's new location."

She slung the camera strap over her shoulder, grabbed her supper, and headed inside. Sitting at the island in the kitchen, she opened the container of food and picked at it. Now, after seeing her aunt's sweater and the unsigned contract, the food she brought home had lost its appeal. Tammy grabbed her keys and purse and left to follow the sheriff to the Sawyer Realty office.

The cruiser was still out front of the business when Tammy pulled in and parked in the lot across the street. Using her binoculars, she had a good view of the standoff through the front window. A few people here and there, who were out on summer's night strolls, watched her as she spied through her binoculars. They stopped to see what she was looking at across the street. The sheriff was standing there holding handcuffs, and Wilmont Sawyer was waving his hands wildly in the air. She could tell he was yelling at the sheriff in protest.

Sawyer finally calmed down and was led out the door. He was put in the back seat of the cruiser, handcuff-free. Tammy could see the receptionist on the phone and assumed she was calling his attorney to meet him at the station. As Zeke was getting in the front seat of the cruiser, he waved to her over the roof of the car so the sheriff wouldn't see him do it.

I can't believe he knew I was here.

Tammy tossed the pulled pork sandwich in the trash when she got home: another meal not eaten. She had to stop wasting good food. A banana and peanut butter sandwich, along with a glass of milk, was quickly substituted for the discarded pork. The news was on, and she plopped in the recliner to watch the weather. It was calling for rain all the next day.

"I should have... bought a pair of boots... when I was shopping," she said, in between using her tongue to remove the peanut butter and bread which was stuck on the roof of her mouth.

Making a cup of tea after finishing her sandwich, she sat out on the porch, just catching the last phase of the sunset. It had become one of her favorite things to do, and it seemed to relax her as she sat there getting lost in the colors of the sky.

She wondered what Wilmont Sawyer was saying at the police station. How could he even dare to deny he was involved when her aunt's things were found on one of his properties? The more she thought about how she believed him the last time they spoke at the real estate office, the angrier she got that she could be taken in so easily by such a snake.

Not feeling much like writing and happy she wasn't working under a deadline at the moment, she riffled through her aunt's front hall closet, looking for a raincoat she could borrow for the following day. She found a bright purple slicker and laughed as she couldn't picture her aunt in any other color. Hanging it on the back of the chair in the kitchen, she accepted the fact she would have totally drenched feet while out searching for her aunt.

Making sure the homemade alarms were all still in place, she flipped on the outside lights and secured the doors. This was the earliest she had been to bed in a long time, but her brain was tired, and she was physically wiped out. She hadn't done much during the day but worrying about her aunt was exhausting her.

She had just settled into bed when her cell phone rang on the nightstand next to her. Zeke called to let her know Wilmont Sawyer denied everything. He claimed he hadn't been back to the drive-in since closing on the property and had no idea how those items ended up there. He also informed her the sheriff was keeping Sawyer locked up for at least twenty-four hours on suspicion of kidnapping. It would buy them the time they needed to get another search warrant for all his properties a second time. The sheriff didn't want the suspect to be able to move her in the middle of the night.

Zeke confirmed he would still be picking her up at ten, and they would split the list with the sheriff and other on-duty deputies to search the large number of holdings Wilmont Sawyer controlled. She promised him coffee in the morning, and they said goodnight.

Tammy hung the two new bird feeders she purchased and filled them with seed while waiting for Zeke to arrive. It didn't take long for the birds to find them. Even in the pouring rain, the feeders were a popular spot. She threw some shelled peanuts on the ground, and the squirrels were busy running around, grabbing what they could and running off with their prizes.

Tammy was waiting on the front porch with two travel mugs of coffee when Zeke pulled up. She crawled into the front seat of the truck and was met with sloppy kisses from Blinky, who was in the back seat of the king cab.

"Blinky, down," Zeke commanded.

"It's okay. I love my kisses. Is he helping us in the search?"

"I have been working with him trying to train him in search and rescue. I figured this would be a good chance to see what he has learned so far.

Can you do me a favor and go back inside and grab something Clara wore recently so Blinky can get her scent?"

"Would slippers work? They are at the side of her bed, and she wears them every day."

"That would be perfect," Zeke said, opening the travel mug. "Could you put them in a plastic bag, please?"

"Sure, I'll be right back."

Before she returned to the truck, she took off her aunt's raincoat as she didn't want to confuse the dog and have him keep returning to the purple slicker because it smelled like her aunt. She put on a windbreaker she had bought the day before. It was lightweight and not very warm, but it was supposed to be waterproof.

Blinky had his head out the window, ready to go for a ride. Zeke handed Tammy the paper he had received from the sheriff earlier in the morning. There were five properties on the list they had to search before Wilmont Sawyer was released from jail and could possibly move Clara again.

It was not going to be easy traipsing through the woods in the rain. At times, it was so torrential you couldn't see your hand in front of your face. Zeke pulled into a dirt road that seemed to get narrower and more overgrown the further they traveled down it. When the truck couldn't go any further, Zeke pulled over and parked.

"Are you ready? The cabin is about a quarter of a mile down that small trail," he said, pointing to an almost invisible path.

"It doesn't look like anyone has used it in quite a while. Is there any other way into the cabin?"

"Not that I know of," he replied. "I'm going to leave Blinky here for this one. The other cabins on the list take much shorter treks to get to. He'll lie down and sleep while we are gone. That is, unless you want to stay here with him, and I'll go by myself."

"No way. I'm in," she answered, grabbing the door handle.

"Blinky, stay," Zeke said, opening his door.

The dog curled up on his blanket and the couple started into the woods. Tammy's sneakers were soaked in no time at all, and the so-called waterproof coat did not perform as it claimed it would. By the time they reached the cabin, they were both a wet mess.

It appeared no one had been to the cabin for years. The brush had overtaken the building, many of the windows were broken, and the chimney had collapsed into the wall of the structure, leaving a gaping hole. They peered into the glassless windows and saw nothing.

"I don't think anyone has been here except for some wild animals," Tammy said, heading around the corner of the rundown cabin.

The door was hanging off its hinges and opened easily. As the couple walked around, a scratching sound startled them. A raccoon had made its home in the fireplace and didn't like intruders in his space. He stood on his back legs, hissed several times, and ran out the open door into the rain.

"It's obvious Clara hasn't been kept here. What say we retreat to the truck and move on to the next spot on the list?" Zeke suggested. "I think the raccoon wants his house back."

As they walked away, they saw the raccoon scoot in the door and return to his dry home. Blinky was looking out the window, waiting for his owner to return. His butt end wiggled up a storm, and he let out little noises like he was saying hello as they got in the truck.

"Good job guarding the truck," Zeke praised him as he scratched behind his ears. "Ready to go for another ride?"

The next three stops were the same as the first one. They were hunting cabins that hadn't been used in a long time by Sawyer or anyone else. Tammy figured the realtor must be sitting on the land for future development. The final stop was a cabin on a well-developed lakefront. It was in excellent condition, had a boat tied up at the dock, and was currently being used. The couple could see unpacked groceries on the kitchen table as they searched from window to window.

"I bet Sawyer uses this on the weekends, or he rents it out," Zeke surmised, standing on the porch and perusing the surrounding area. "I don't think he would hide Clara here as there are too many people around enjoying the lake during the summer season."

"Just to be on the safe side, why don't you get Blinky out of the truck, let him sniff the slippers, and see if he reacts to anything," Tammy suggested.

"Even if it's raining, he should still be able to pick up a scent if Clara has been here."

Zeke attached Blinky's harness and leash and let him out of the truck. He gave him the slippers to sniff and gave the command to search. The couple followed the dog around in the rain while he sniffed anything and everything in his path, but he didn't react or give the signal of sitting down, showing he had picked up the missing woman's scent.

"I guess she was never here either," Tammy said, sighing.

"Don't lose hope. Remember, Blinky is still in training, and this is the first time he has searched in the rain. Come on, I'll drop you off at home and call the sheriff to tell him we found nothing at any of the properties on our list."

He put Blinky in the back seat, and they no sooner settled into their seats up front when the dog shook, covering them and the inside of the truck with secondhand rain.

"Blinky! Really?" Zeke said as the dog laid his head on the back of the seat and looked at them with pitiful eyes.

Tammy started laughing.

"Look at that face and those eyes. Can't you tell he is *so* sorry? Besides, we can't get any wetter than we are already."

"That's true," Zeke said, joining in on the laughter. "We do look pretty bad."

"Let's go home, dry out, and then go out to supper. You game?"

"As long as we go somewhere that serves clam chowder. I am in the mood for a huge bowl of steaming hot chowder to warm up my insides," he said, putting the truck in gear.

"That sounds really good."

Tammy opened the console compartment in between them to see if there were any napkins to wipe off the water running down her nose. Instead, she spotted a ring box and assumed it held the ring he was going to give Emily. She closed the console, and they rode back to town in silence.

"Is something bothering you? You got awful quiet during the ride home," Zeke asked, turning into her aunt's driveway.

"Yeah, I just don't know how to approach the subject," she admitted.

"You know you can talk to me about anything. What is it? Are you worried about Clara?"

"I am worried about my aunt but it's not that, it's something else. You never told me how your meeting went with Emily. Did she accept the fact you have moved on and didn't want to get back together with her?"

"I wasn't keeping it a secret. I just didn't think about it again after I left the café. She understood my side and agreed she had to move on, too. She asked if we could still be cordial to each other as she would be staying in town to take care of her mother, and she didn't want any scenes in public if we ran into each other."

"So, it's over?"

"Yes, it is," he said, putting the truck in park. "Do you feel better now?"

"Why is her ring still in your truck? If it is her ring?"

"You're right; it is hers, or it was. I put it in the console the day after she left it on my kitchen counter because I was going to try to return it, but the jeweler wouldn't take it back. It's been sitting in there ever since. I meant to put it in my safe but never got around to doing it."

"I must sound like a jealous schoolgirl," Tammy mumbled.

"It's flattering, actually," he said, smiling. "Emily never got upset when I talked to other women. I should have told you about the outcome of our meeting, and I apologize."

"Accepted. I will never bring it up again. Clean slate from here on out, I promise. Pick me up in an hour?" she asked, opening the truck door.

"See you then."

After checking the answering machine for any new messages, she took the hottest shower she could stand to warm up. Even though it was summer, the rain had cooled down the air, so Tammy donned a sweater she had bought for Fall use. She still had half an hour before Zeke arrived, so she put in a call to her agent, and they chatted about the pages and the synopsis she had sent him. He liked the new book and had already started shopping around the concept to see if there was any interest in it from the publishers of her past books.

He hadn't heard anything back yet but promised her he would let her know if he did. Tammy was upfront and honest with him, saying she hadn't been writing as much as she should have been with her aunt's disappearance, and she would try to do better. He asked her to draw up a timeline and send it to him so he had some kind of idea of when it would be complete in case he was asked. She promised to get it to him in the next few days.

Zeke picked her up, and after a short discussion, they decided instead of going to the Brown Bear Café, which was their usual hangout, they would go to the Fulton Diner instead. Zeke had eaten there many times before his bowling league and had nothing but praise for the clam chowder there.

The parking lot at the diner was full, so Zeke parked across the street in the church parking lot. As Tammy hopped down from the truck, she noticed a car several spots away, which looked familiar.

"Doesn't that look like Toby Brown's car?" she asked.

"It does, but I'm sure there is more than one of that type of vehicle in the area," Zeke said.

"You're right. Let's go eat."

The diner was split into various-sized rooms. Booths lined the perimeter of each area while two tops and four tops filled in the center sections. The hostess recognized Zeke and asked him if he wanted his regular booth. Once seated, they glanced over the menus and perused the special board on the wall.

"Is there any eating establishment you aren't known at by name?" Tammy asked.

"Probably not. I told you I eat out all the time. Any restaurant within a half hour's travel time is fair game. I like to change things up and try various kinds of food, but when I find a place I like, I keep eating there."

"Hello, Zeke," the older waitress said as she approached their table. "What will it be tonight? Wait a minute, it's not your bowling night. Are you and this pretty lady here on a date?"

"I guess you could call it that," he smiled. "Actually, I was craving some of your famous clam chowder and talked her into coming here with me to try it. Tammy, Alice. Alice, Tammy."

"Nice to meet you, Tammy."

"Nice to meet you, too."

"So, I am assuming we are starting with two cups of chowder?" she asked, flipping open her order pad.

"Not on your life. We need bowls of chowder, not cups. And extra oyster crackers, please," Zeke requested. "Are you ready to order, Tammy?"

"Yes, I am. I'm going to try the sausage gravy and biscuits, please."

"Corn, green beans, or summer squash?"

"Summer squash and a large root beer," Tammy requested.

"And are you having your regular," she asked, turning to Zeke.

"Yes, ma'am."

"Okay. I'll be back with your chowder and drinks," she said, picking up the closed menus.

"Spill. What is your regular?"

"Every Saturday night, I have their country-fried steak and homemade mashed potatoes. The gravy is some of the best I've ever eaten."

Alice returned with their chowder. As they ate, they discussed what Zeke had found out when talking to the sheriff earlier. All sixteen places Wilmont Sawyer owned had been checked, and Clara hadn't been found at any of them, nor had there been any sign she had even been there. After Zeke's call to clear the places on his list, the sheriff said he was going to have to release Sawyer.

Their next discussion was centered on where Tammy was going to live once they found Clara and she returned home. It was something she hadn't really thought about until Zeke brought it up.

"I guess I can stay with my aunt until I figure something out," she said.

"There are some really nice houses for sale in the area which are still reasonably priced."

"And Sawyer or Flashpoint Realty hasn't snapped them up yet?"

"They are only interested in large tracks of land or good-sized lots they can join together to form an area big enough for development. They don't want individual lots in already established neighborhoods. And from what I have seen, most of the houses up for sale are being sold by the owners themselves and not through an agency."

"They don't trust Sawyer. Is that what you are saying?"

"That's right, and the only other option is Flashpoint. People around here trust Brown even less than they do Sawyer."

"Maybe I should get my real estate license. I'd make a killing with no one else around the locals trust," Tammy laughed.

"Between your writing career and possibly owning the ceramic shop, I think you'll have enough on your plate."

"Even if I own Idle Chat on paper, it will still be my aunt's shop. Only difference will be I am bankrolling the place and will be able to bring in a couple of extra people to help out my aunt so I can return to my writing. She doesn't have the extra money in her existing budget to hire anyone."

"It sounds like a win-win for everyone. You'll still need a place to live because of your decision to stay here permanently and no cottage to live in because of the fire."

"I do, and I think I will be looking for a place like my aunt's. I don't want close neighbors who can see every move I make. After living in such close quarters in the city, privacy is very important to me. I want a big yard with surrounding woods so I can continue to feed my wildlife with no one complaining about it."

"Sounds like you know exactly what you want."

"Well, until my aunt returns home safely all of this is on the back burner. I have to concentrate on finding her."

Alice returned to take away their empty chowder bowls and deliver their meals. Tammy ordered another root beer as the diner served the old-fashioned kind that had a bite to it, and she hadn't had any like it in years.

The discussion during dinner turned to likes and dislikes, hobbies, and family. The two finished catching up on everything that had happened in their lives over the last six years. By the time they ordered dessert, it was as if time had stood still and the years they were apart had never happened.

Tammy was taking the last bite of her strawberry shortcake when she noticed Toby Brown sitting in a corner booth, which was half hidden by one of the columns covered in mirrored tiles. In the reflection of the tiles, she could see the man's face whose back was to her and was sitting with Brown.

He had a full beard and mustache and straight, shoulder-length black hair.

As Tammy was staring at the reflection, Brown slid to the end of the booth and spotted her. The man with him shoved a ballcap on his head, pulling it down as low as he could before he got up and ran for the rear of the restaurant. He must have exited through an alarmed door and not the regular exit, as the fire alarm sounded and people ran for the street. Brown followed right behind his friend.

"What's happening?" Zeke asked.

"Head for Toby Brown's car," Tammy yelled, taking off for the front door.

By the time they managed to get out the door and through the rush of people, the car was gone. The fire department quickly descended on the diner, and the firemen disappeared inside. The patrons stood outside waiting for the fire department to give the all-clear signal to return to their meals. While they waited, Tammy explained to the fire chief what she witnessed and what had caused the alarm to go off. He thanked her and went to round up his crew to leave.

The couple returned to retrieve their bill and pay it as they were done eating. Alice thanked them for coming back in as she had several tables in her section, which were empty except for the half-eaten meals because the customers did not return to finish or pay their bills. Zeke felt bad for the waitress and gave her double the tip he usually left.

"Tell me about this guy you saw sitting with Brown," Zeke said, pulling out of the parking lot.

"I couldn't really see his facial features. He had a dark brown or black beard, moustache, and shoulder-length hair. As he ran away, I could see he was of medium build and maybe six feet tall."

"I can't think of anyone in town who fits that description," Zeke said.

"Well, whoever he was, he didn't want to be seen. I bet the guy who took off was Brown's silent partner."

"Could be. Maybe they thought they were far enough away from Braddock and they wouldn't run into anyone they knew. You were probably the last person he figured would be eating there."

"I don't think he'll be dining there again," Tammy stated. "Maybe we should go out to eat every night when you don't work and look for them. I bet his friend lives over here in Fulton and not in Braddock."

"He might. I'm not saying I know everyone in Braddock, but a person like him I would remember. I'll have to ask the sheriff if he knows anyone fitting his description."

Zeke turned on the radio, and Tammy watched out the window for Brown's car. Ten minutes later, they pulled into Clara's driveway. He waited until she got inside the cabin, and she watched him drive away through the safety of the locked door.

As she always did, her first stop was the answering machine. The red light was flashing.

Chapter Ten

"Please be Aunt Clara," she said, pushing the rewind button.

It was not Clara as Tammy had wished it had been. It was Wilmont Sawyer, and he sounded pretty desperate. He swore up and down it was not him who had kidnapped Clara and requested a meeting with her at his office the following day at eleven o'clock.

Why would he want to see me?

Tammy lay in bed for a long time before finally falling asleep. She tossed and turned all night. In her dreams she was running away from a figure who had no face or legs but had long black hair. He floated behind her, his arms reaching out but never quite getting close enough to actually grab her. In the next second, she could hear her aunt calling out to her as she was being dragged away by the same unknown figure. Her eyes sprung open, and she sat straight up in bed. Her breathing was shallow, and her heartbeat rapid.

Afraid to go back to sleep, knowing she would probably have the same dream, she got up to make herself a cup of tea. Sitting in the dark at three o'clock in the morning, sipping her drink, she heard a loud thud come from the back porch area. Grabbing her aunt's frying pan, she made her way through the kitchen to the back door. Checking the door to make sure it was locked and the deadbolt was in place, she peeked out from behind the curtain covering the door's window.

Tammy didn't see anything moving around in the brightness of the spotlight lighting up the back yard. Deciding to take a chance, she unlocked the door and stepped outside, the frying pan poised above her head. In her peripheral vision, she saw something black heading toward her from the far end of the porch. Letting out a scream, she ran back into the cabin and quickly relocked the door.

Sliding down the wall, she sat on the floor, catching her breath. Tammy could hear movement on the other side of the door. Mustering up all the courage she could, she stood up, flipped the curtain open, screamed go away, and waved the frying pan around as if threatening whoever was outside.

She almost had a heart attack when a huge bear stood up on its rear legs, let out a growl, and looked right in the window at her. It was the first bear she had ever seen in real life, and it looked twice as big as they did on television. Tammy had heard them outside the cottage trying to get at the trash barrels locked in the shed but had never come face to face with one. Luckily, he didn't seem as interested in her as he was in finding some food. He dropped to all fours, wandered off through the backyard, and then into the woods out of sight. She let out a deep sigh.

What a really stupid move going out on the porch in the middle of the night. Tammy, you have got to think before you act. I am definitely a city girl and never even considered a bear would be out there. Now I really need that cup of tea.

After nuking her tea to warm it up, she dozed off on the couch before finishing it.

Up early, Tammy went to check on the ceramic shop as she hadn't been there for a while. She walked the perimeter, and nothing seemed out of place or disturbed. Once inside, she walked from room to room and the same was apparent.

The blood was still on the concrete floor near the back loading dock. She still hadn't cleaned up after the murder and had to get it done before her aunt returned. Another thought entered her head, and she walked to the kiln room.

Opening the large kiln Goodwin had been stuffed into, there were blood stains on the inside walls and metal coils where his head had rested. If it was fired, there could be an awful smell from the residue burning off in the high temperature.

Tammy closed the cover and put a low-burning cone in the timer. She would let it burn the first time while no one was there. Then, she would return over the next two days, staying each time during the process to see if the smell would dissipate after multiple firings. If not, she would have to dispose of the kiln.

Checking her watch, she had twenty minutes to get to town for her meeting with Wilmont Sawyer. Traffic was light as it was a perfect beach day, and most of the tourists were probably out at Fulton Point enjoying the sunshine and warm water. She slid into her parking space with ten minutes to spare.

Watching from her car, she noticed how quiet the realty office was, with no one going in or coming out. Looking through her trusty binoculars, she could see the place was empty. The receptionist wasn't even at her desk.

Strange. It's almost as if the place is closed.

At eleven o'clock on the dot, she entered the office. She could hear Wilmont Sawyer talking on the phone in one of the back offices. Not wanting to walk back there and appear rude, she waited in the reception area, perusing the family pictures hanging on the wall. She was stopped in front of a picture that showed a young man in a military uniform when Wilmont came from the back room.

"That's my oldest son, Mark," he said proudly. "He's been overseas for almost two years serving in the army."

"I bet you miss him."

"Not as much as his mom does. She worries about him all the time. He's supposed to be home on leave shortly after Christmas."

"That will be a nice family reunion."

"Not if the sheriff doesn't find Clara alive and well," he said, frowning.

"And this picture. I swear I have seen him somewhere before."

"That's my youngest, Kenny. He works at the feed and grain store here in town."

"That's where I have seen him. I buy my bird food there."

"He's the only one left in Braddock. His mom is happy because she still has one of her children living at home. If this kidnapping charge isn't straightened out, he may be the only one she has at home with her."

"Why did you want to see me, Mr. Sawyer?"

"I need you to believe me. I would never hurt Clara no matter how much I wanted her land."

"But the contract and her sweater were found on property you own. How do you explain that?"

"I can't. The only plausible idea I can come up with is someone is trying to frame me, and I think that someone is Toby Brown."

"Why would Toby Brown want to frame you?"

"Think about it. He wants me out of the way because we are both trying to purchase the same properties. He beat me out of the old Grady mansion and the vacant lot next to it. Now, from what I hear, he is harassing Hattie Cotton to sell her property."

"He is," Tammy confirmed. "But give me a good reason why I should believe you don't have my aunt hidden somewhere."

"Because, unlike Toby Brown, I have moved on and purchased a large amount of acreage just outside of town to build my condo development. I'm going to put a mini mall on the vacant drive-in land, and that's where my two main focuses are right now."

"It doesn't mean you didn't take her before you changed your mind," Tammy insisted.

"You sound like the sheriff," Sawyer grumbled.

"In my defense, you have to look at this from my side. You threatened my aunt and me, you destroyed the windows in her car laughing while you did it and threatened to chase away all her customers to destroy her business."

"In *my* defense, I put a bid in on the twenty-three acres three days before your aunt disappeared. I signed the agreement to purchase the land the morning before Clara was taken."

"The only thing Toby Brown ever did was send my aunt a letter from Flashpoint Realty saying they were interested in buying the shop and land. He never called her or even approached her in person. More important, he never bullied my aunt before she disappeared like you did," Tammy said.

"I saw Brown at Clara's shop twice before you arrived here."

"She never mentioned he had been there. She only showed me the letter he sent to her after I arrived."

"It doesn't mean he wasn't there at some point."

"True. I'll ask you again. Why did you ask me here?"

"Truthfully, I don't trust the sheriff to do a complete investigation. He would love nothing better than to pin this kidnapping on me. I want to hire you, under the table of course. No one has to know you are working for me. I want you to watch Toby Brown and all he does."

"I am not a licensed private investigator," Tammy stated.

"I know. But you have a good head on your shoulders, and I get the impression you can be fair and impartial, unlike Sheriff Becker."

"I don't want your money, Mr. Sawyer. Anything I do will have one specific reason and it is to find my aunt. You are still not off my radar, you or Toby Brown."

"That's fair and upfront. I really need your help to prove I am innocent, and I will do whatever I can to help you reach that conclusion."

"I need you to be completely honest with me. While you were in jail, several of us searched every property you own looking for my aunt. I need to know if there are any other properties in other names where my aunt could be."

Sawyer walked to a file cabinet behind the receptionist's desk and rummaged through the top drawer. He randomly pulled out folders here and there and then closed the drawer.

"This is every property I own. Some under my name and some under a corporate name. If you don't believe me, my records are yours to go through whenever you like," he said, handing her the files.

"May I take these home with me?"

"Yes, but please be extremely careful with them. I wouldn't want my business dealings to be made public. I especially don't want them to fall into Toby Brown's hands."

"I can see you trust me and really want my help. Do you have an office I can use to look through the files and make a list of the properties we haven't searched through yet? I won't remove the files from your office, and I will keep everything I learn from them confidential unless the information leads to finding my aunt, and then I will have to tell the sheriff."

"Fair enough. Take your pick. Ever since word got out I was brought in for questioning about Clara's things being found at the drive-in, I haven't had a single soul cross my doorstep. I've even had a few listings pulled from my office. Everyone who works here was sent home for some time off until Clara is found, and it's proved I'm innocent."

"Fine. I'll use this first office. It shouldn't take me more than an hour," Tammy said, picking up the stack of file folders.

"I'll be in my office. Second door on the right if you need anything."

As Tammy glanced through the files, she wondered if Sawyer was upfront with her and if this was indeed all the properties he owned. She still didn't trust him enough to take his word for anything. When she was done, she had a list of nine additional places. She walked back to Sawyer's office and poked her head in the door.

"I left the files on the table. I'll be in touch."

"I'm not going anywhere. Just here and home," he said as the phone rang. "Excuse me, I have to take this."

Sitting in her car, Tammy perused the list she had compiled. Seven of the nine properties were located in Fulton. She could go check them out herself but knew she needed Blinky's sniffing ability in case Clara had been there and was moved.

She called Zeke to see what his next day off was so they could bring the dog to check the new list of places in Fulton. He worked for the next three days, and Tammy didn't want to wait that long. Listening to his last words warning her to wait until he could accompany her and that she needed to turn the new listings over to the sheriff, she said goodbye.

Returning to the cabin, she worked on her new book for the rest of the afternoon and into the night. Closing her computer at nine o'clock, she showered and went to bed.

Visiting the ceramic shop for a second day, Tammy set the kiln on a low burn again. There were still some blood stains on the inside, but they weren't as bad as they had been the day before. She kept busy trying to clean up the blood off the loading dock floor while the kiln heated up, but it had soaked into the concrete, and the existing stains were not going to go away.

Maybe I can get Zeke to help me paint the floor with a color-infused concrete sealer so Aunt Clara won't see the blood stains.

While she was scrubbing several plot twists came to mind for her new book. She was anxious to get back to the cabin and enter them into her computer before she forgot what they were. This book was going to be so much better than her others as it would have more of an emotional truth to it from the victim's families' points of view. Getting words on her computer to send her agent was what she needed to do instead of traipsing around on her own, checking out the properties, and putting herself in possible danger. She called the sheriff and gave him the new listings.

Now you're using your brain.

There was a faint smell coming from the kiln. Tammy figured with a few more firings no one would be able to tell what happened on the dreadful day when Goodwin died.

She was walking across the parking lot to her car when she heard loud arguing coming from just beyond the bushes separating the shop property and Hattie Cotton's place. Peering through the branches, she saw Toby Brown standing on the sidewalk in front of Hattie's house, and the elderly woman was out front yelling at him.

Tammy ran down the street and jumped up on the porch, joining Hattie and her sister, who had just come out of the house.

"Get him away from my house," Hattie screamed.

"This is a public sidewalk. You can't tell me where to stand and where not to stand," he yelled back. "Quit your squawking old lady."

"Knowing your mama like I do, I can't believe she didn't teach you any manners growing up," Hattie stated fiercely. "Oh wait! She probably did, but you're just a low-life, no-class person."

"This is what I deal with almost every day," Mabel whispered to Tammy.

Tammy walked down off the porch and stood directly in front of Toby Brown.

"What are you trying to accomplish here, Mr. Brown, besides being rude and ill-mannered to someone who is twice your age?" she demanded.

"Mind your own business," he snarled.

"You made it my business when you insulted Hattie," she fired back, showing no fear.

"If she'd just sell me this old ramshackle house, I wouldn't have to talk to her anymore," he yelled loud enough for Hattie to hear.

"She's made it quite clear she will not sell to you, so why don't you back off and leave her alone?"

"I'm not letting an old lady stand in my way of success. If I have to stand here every day and wear her down, that's what I'll do."

"Let's see what the sheriff has to say about that," Tammy said, pulling out her cell phone.

"Meddling New Yorker. Why don't you go back to where you came from?"

"Unfortunately for you, Mr. Brown, I am back to where I came from, and I have no intention of leaving any time soon. Sheriff Becker, please."

"You'll pay for this," he threatened just as the sheriff answered the phone and heard what was being said.

"Who is this?" the sheriff demanded.

"It's Tammy Wright. I am at Hattie Cotton's house, and we need the police to come here to diffuse a situation caused by Toby Brown."

"Was that him I just heard threatening you?"

"Yes, it was, and apparently, he stands out here in front of Hattie's house every day to harass her into selling her property."

"We'll be there as soon as we can."

"Thank you," Tammy said, hitting the button, ending her call. "The sheriff will be here shortly. Do you still want to stick around, Mr. Brown?"

"You think you're all that, don't you? You'll get yours along with those two, I'll make sure of it," he threatened, leaning in, and getting right in her face.

"Keep talking. I am recording and got everything you just said on my phone. I think the sheriff will be really interested in this video if something happens to any one of us. Don't you?"

"Give me that phone," he demanded, trying to wrestle it out of her hand.

She kept a tight grip on it and proceeded to put her self-defense moves into action, the ones she had learned in New York to defend herself when walking around alone at night in the city. Tammy stomped on the top of his foot as hard as she could. He let out a yelp and released his grip on her hand and the phone. Shoving him down on the sidewalk, she ran to the porch steps.

The siren signaled the approaching cruiser. Brown got up and ran as best as he could with his hurt foot. Hopping in his car, he took off in the opposite direction of the incoming police.

"Where is he?" the sheriff asked out the car window.

"He drove toward the drive-in," Hattie said.

"I'll be back," he said, taking off after the suspect.

"Brown is going to be furious now," Hattie said. "I believe I need to get my husband's old shotgun out of the attic and keep it downstairs."

"Let's not overreact," Mabel told her sister. "You shouldn't even be talking such nonsense unless you are serious about using it if the need arises."

"Oh, I'll use it, okay. My husband didn't teach me to shoot if he didn't mean for me to defend myself," she claimed.

"I think I'd ask the sheriff what he thinks about the idea first," Tammy advised. "You don't want to spend your final days in jail because of an accidental shooting."

"Oh, believe me, it wouldn't be an accident. A person can only be pushed so far, and with Brown, I have reached my limit," Hattie stated emphatically. "Coming here every day and yelling at me from the sidewalk, he's got a lot of nerve and no class."

"I'd still talk to the sheriff to see what other avenues you could pursue," Tammy insisted.

"I'll hide the gun," Mabel whispered to Tammy. "She won't be able to find it."

"Good idea," Tammy whispered out of the side of her mouth. "Now, I need to get some writing done on my next book. I will see you ladies later."

"Just so you know, we do keep an eye on Clara's shop while no one is there," Hattie said.

"I appreciate it, and so does my aunt," she said, walking down the path.

Tammy was at her computer when Zeke called. He was off work at three and asked if she wanted to go to Fulton and try a different restaurant to see if Brown and his friend had started eating elsewhere. She agreed, and he said he would pick her up at six. This gave the author four hours to buckle down and get some writing done.

Six-thirty rolled around, and no Zeke. He was usually punctual, so Tammy called him to make sure he was all right. His phone rang but went straight to voicemail. She texted him and got no reply. Not knowing anyone else except the sheriff to call, all she could do was sit and wait.

To keep herself from staring at the clock, she opened her computer to write but found she couldn't concentrate. Her fingers sat on the keys while she stared blankly at the screen. Every twenty to thirty minutes, she tried to call Zeke but got the same results each time.

Where are you, Zeke?

Her stomach growled.

It's too late to go out to supper now. I guess I'll make myself some supper.

Waiting for her soup to heat up, she dialed Zeke's number again. This time, someone answered.

"Hello."

"Sheriff, what are you doing answering Zeke's phone?"

Chapter Eleven

"Tammy, is that you?"

"Yes, it is. Where is Zeke, and why do you have his phone?"

"I'm at the mall. Someone found Zeke's truck in the parking lot, door open, his phone on the floor of the front seat, and called it in. When did you last talk to him?"

"Just after two. He called to see if I wanted to go out to supper with him. He was supposed to pick me up at six but never showed up. I called him at six-thirty but got no answer."

"He was at work until three. If he had gone home to change and then come to the mall, that would have been another half hour. It appears he had just put his purchases on the front seat when something happened to him. So, whatever took place had to have occurred after three-thirty and before six o'clock."

"Where was his truck parked?" Tammy asked.

"At the back of the mall."

"Near Flashpoint Realty?"

"About a hundred yards away. Why do you ask?"

"I'm wondering if Zeke saw something he shouldn't have seen, like Brown's silent partner leaving the office. He wouldn't have left his phone behind, especially on the floor of the truck with the door open so someone could walk off with it."

"The keys were on the ground next to the truck. He could have been attempting to get in and was hit from behind," the sheriff surmised.

"I don't like this. First Aunt Clara and now Zeke. If he doesn't show up shortly someone will have to get Blinky and take care of him," Tammy said.

"I have an extra key to Zeke's house from the last time I took care of the dog. I can bring Blinky to my house. He gets along with my two dogs and has always been good while visiting," the sheriff said. "But let's not get ahead of ourselves and think the worst."

"Zeke is always so dependable, though. If he says he's going to be somewhere, he is."

"I know it doesn't look good but there may be another explanation to why he's gone."

"If he calls me, I'll call you immediately," Tammy promised.

"Good, and I'll keep you up to date if I learn anything."

"Please do."

Tammy took her mug of tomato soup and sat in her aunt's recliner. She felt numb and so alone. One by one she was losing those she cared for and those she loved. Several sips of soup later, her pity-me thoughts disappeared, and her survival instinct kicked in. Now, she was angry.

Everything seems to revolve around Flashpoint Realty. If Wilmont Sawyer has really moved on and is going to build his condos somewhere else, it leaves only Toby Brown and his need for the local properties. But why is it so important to keep the identity of his silent partner secret.

Mindlessly flipping through the channels and not finding anything interesting on TV, she shut it off and stared into space. There had to be something she was missing, but what was it?

Starting at the beginning, she pieced together everything that had happened since she had arrived back in Braddock. No matter what event she rehashed, the two names she always came back to: Wilmont Sawyer and Toby Brown.

One point that bothered her was no one but herself, Zeke, and Aunt Clara knew she had offered to buy the ceramic shop. But it was summertime, and all the windows were open when she first discussed the subject with her aunt. Several times men were lurking near the cabin, and anyone could have been outside listening and heard their conversation.

So, was Clara kidnapped to prevent her from selling the shop to her niece or was she taken to scare her into submission to selling to whoever had her, and they found the contract by accident when they broke into her cabin? Either way, the kidnappers had seen the contract and knew of Tammy's plan to buy Idle Chat.

Then it hit her. The guy she saw attempting to crawl in the window at the back of the cabin could have been the same man she saw sitting with Toby Brown at the diner in Fulton. He had the same facial hair and was the same build. Unfortunately, she hadn't been near enough either time to confirm what she was thinking.

Her head was aching from the stress of worrying about her aunt, and now Zeke. Trying to figure out who was behind their disappearances was mentally exhausting. Frustration set in for the author because everything seemed so easy to put together and solve in her books. Faced with dealing with real-life criminal acts, she came to the realization that not only did her characters have to change but so did her way of creating the solutions to make the books more realistic. Her books were good but now they had to be better.

Here I am worrying about my writing when two people are missing and could possibly be dead. Sometimes, you're such a jerk, Tammy.

Shortly after midnight, she fell asleep in the recliner. In the wee hours of the morning, she was startled out of a sound sleep when she heard the trash barrels crashing around on the back porch.

This time don't open the door, you idiot. It must be another bear.

She flipped on the rear porch light, hoping to scare the animal away. Peeking through the curtains, she discovered it wasn't a bear searching for food. Zeke was lying in the middle of the turned-over barrels and not moving. She ran for her phone to call an ambulance.

"Zeke! Can you hear me?" she asked, tossing the cans off the porch. "Yes, I need an ambulance at 171 Pine Tree Lane."

Zeke groaned but didn't open his eyes.

"Yes, he's breathing. He looks like he has a head injury. Please hurry. We are out on the back porch of the cabin."

Tammy knew it was the middle of the night, but she called the sheriff anyway.

"Hello," the sheriff mumbled. "This better be good."

"Sheriff Becker, it's me, Tammy Wright. I am so sorry to call you this time of night, but Zeke just showed up on my aunt's back porch and is unconscious. I called an ambulance, and they are on their way."

"Is he badly injured?"

"It looks like he was whacked in the head. He also has remnants of duct tape around one of his wrists."

"I'll be right over."

The space around Zeke had been cleared, and Tammy was cradling his head and talking to him when the ambulance arrived.

"We're out here," she yelled.

She stepped aside as the paramedics took over.

"Was he conscious when you found him?"

"No, he groaned once, but other than that, he's just been lying there."

"Let's get him on the gurney and get his vitals. Zeke, can you hear me, buddy?"

No response.

"We need to get him to the hospital as quickly as possible for x-rays. He's got a really nasty blow to the back of the head."

"Tammy!" the sheriff yelled.

"Back here," she answered.

"How is he?" the sheriff asked the paramedics.

"There is no response. We need to transport him now."

"Okay. I'll be at the hospital shortly in case he comes to," the sheriff replied.

Tammy and the sheriff stood in the driveway, watching the ambulance drive away. She teared up and tried to wipe the tears away before Sheriff Becker could see her crying. He put a fatherly arm around her shoulders and waited until she finished before asking her any questions.

"Did you see where he came from?"

"I was asleep and didn't know he was out there until he crashed into the trash cans."

"I don't think he could have traveled very far in his condition. He must

116

have been being held somewhere close by. When I get to the station, I will run a check on who owns the properties in the immediate area. Right now, I'm going to head to the hospital and check on my deputy."

Tammy could see he was visibly shaken over what had happened to Zeke. The two men had known each other for many years and had become even closer working together.

"Are you okay?" she asked.

"Yeah, I'm okay. I'm furious as to what is happening in my quiet little town. First Clara, and now this. Zeke is like a son to me. I cheered him on while he played football in high school, drank with him through his break-up with Emily, and now I enjoy watching how happy he is being with you. He didn't deserve what was done to him. When I get my hands on whoever is doing these things…"

"Maybe he saw something before he was hit," Tammy suggested.

"I don't know. He was definitely hit from behind, judging by the injury."

"I'm going to lock up and head to the hospital right behind you. They probably won't let me sit in the room with him, but at least I can be in the waiting room if he wakes up," Tammy stated.

"I'm going to check on Zeke's condition and then go drag a couple of people out of bed to ask some questions about where they were tonight."

"I hope the first one is Toby Brown. He needs to tell you who his silent partner is and if they were at the realty office together at the same time, Zeke was at the mall."

"Before I forget, when I returned to check on Hattie and her sister after chasing Brown and losing him, I suggested Hattie Cotton take out a restraining order against Mr. Brown. I also told her to use my name as a witness to get said order."

"I'll gladly add my name to the list as he assaulted me to get my phone away from me when I recorded his threats."

"You have his threats recorded? Wait a minute, he assaulted you?"

"I do, and yes, he did. If it's needed, I'll be there to let the judge hear it," Tammy confirmed.

"And you're not going to press charges against him?"

"I believe I hurt him more than he did me. He might have a few broken bones to deal with," Tammy said. "I used my self-defense training and stomped on the top of his foot pretty hard to make him let me go."

"Good for you, and here I was worried about you," he chuckled. "I'll see you shortly."

Tammy locked the kitchen door. She pondered whether or not to go out and pick up the barrels but thought better of it. Daylight would be a better time to clean up the mess when no wild animals would be around. She got dressed and left for the hospital.

Braddock General was twenty minutes away. She checked with the front desk in the emergency room to see if there was any update on Zeke's condition. There was no word yet, and the desk nurse asked her to wait in the adjacent room.

She grabbed a cup of coffee from the vending machine and sat down with a magazine to read. Her drink tasted terrible, like burnt coffee that had been sitting in the pot for hours, but she drank it anyway, needing a little boost to help her stay awake. Sheriff Becker joined her a short time later. He also grabbed some coffee even though Tammy warned him how bad it tasted. They sat there in silence, staring at the television up on the wall. Time seemed to drag on and the sky's darkness was fading as the sun was starting to rise.

"Harry," the doctor said.

"I'll be right back," the sheriff told her.

Tammy watched the two men converse. The doctor showed the sheriff something on his clipboard, and they both frowned. She knew by their actions that something was not right. She couldn't wait any longer and went to join the conversation.

"Paul, this is Zeke's new girlfriend, Tammy Wright. Tammy, this is Doctor Paul Downey."

Tammy gave the sheriff a funny look.

"Nice to meet you. How is Zeke?" she asked.

"Tammy Wright, the author?"

"Yes."

"I love your books. Clara introduced me to them."

"Thank you. How is Zeke?" she asked again.

"We have put Mr. Peters in a drug-induced coma. Judging by the wound on the back of his head, he must have been hit with a crowbar or something of the same shape and size. He has a fracture on the back right side of his skull, and the injury is causing some swelling of the brain."

"Is there any permanent damage?"

"I don't know as of yet. We'll know better when the swelling goes down and he regains consciousness. Right now, he needs to rest."

"I guess he won't be telling me any time soon if he saw who whacked him," the sheriff surmised. "Paul, please call me the minute he wakes up."

"I will. I'll put it on his chart that you need to be called."

"Can I see him?" Tammy asked. "Only for a minute or two?"

"They haven't got him set up in his ICU room yet. Only immediate family is supposed to be allowed in there."

"His mom and dad are in Florida. I have to call them when I get out of here so they can make the decision to come up or not. Don't you think that if his family is not here, Tammy could visit him? She is his girlfriend," the sheriff said again.

"I guess it will be all right. You'll have to come back in a few hours after we have him settled in but remember you can only stay for five minutes at a time," the doctor advised.

"I promise."

"I'll add your name to the list of approved visitors. Now, I have to get back."

"Thanks, Paul. I'll be waiting to hear from you," the sheriff said.

"I'm glad I picked up Blinky already. I guess he'll be staying with us for a while," the sheriff said when they reached Tammy's car.

"He's going to be so confused not knowing where Zeke is," Tammy said. "Why did you tell the doctor I was Zeke's girlfriend? We're only friends."

"I knew he wouldn't let you in to see Zeke unless I said that, and I know how worried you are about him. As for Blinky, he'll have plenty of doggie company to keep him occupied," the sheriff assured her. "And my wife spoils them all rotten. I swear she spends more on dog treats than she does on food for us to eat."

"Isn't that the way it's supposed to be?"

"I guess so."

"I'm going to pay Mr. Brown a visit and find out where he was yesterday at the time of Zeke's attack. If Paul calls me in regard to Zeke, I will let you know."

"Great, but I'll be here at the hospital until I'm able to go up to ICU. I'm going home to shower and grab my computer so I can write while I'm waiting. The doctor said it would be a while before I can see Zeke, so I have time to go to Idle Chat and check the kiln to see if I need to fire it again to get rid of the smell and the blood stain before my aunt returns."

"Were you able to clean the floor?"

"No, I wasn't. I was going to ask Zeke to help me paint the floor with a colored cement sealer, but now I will have to do it myself tomorrow afternoon."

"Stay positive," the sheriff repeated, walking to his car several spots over from Tammy's.

The red light was blinking on the answering machine when Tammy arrived home. She hit the play button and was surprised at who had left the message.

"Tammy, this is Emily Bosen. News of Zeke's attack has made its way around town. I was told you were staying at Clara's, so I am calling you here for your advice. I would like very much to go see Zeke, but I don't know if it would upset him too much, or you. I know it's over between us, but I still care about him. Please let me know what you think, My number is 703-555-5515."

I suppose you can't just turn off feelings for someone after being with them for six years.

She dialed the number given and it went to Emily's messages. Tammy explained Zeke was in ICU and no one but immediate family could visit with him. She didn't tell her she was being allowed to visit, also. Ending the message with advice to call the sheriff if she needed updates, Tammy hung up.

I think I was pleasant enough.

Her phone quacked, indicating she had received a text. It was from the sheriff advising her Zeke's parents would be flying in later in the day. He was going to pick them up at the airport and bring them right to the hospital if she wanted to visit with them. She texted back, stating she would be there.

Tossing her laptop on the front seat next to her, she left the cabin for the ceramic shop. She locked and alarmed her car with her computer inside. Doing her normal walk around the property to see that nothing was amiss, she spotted a window partially open.

I know I didn't leave it open like that.

Taking a closer look, she noticed jimmy marks along the bottom of the window frame.

Oh, this isn't good.

She made her way to the front door and entered the building. Being as quiet as possible, she searched room by room, looking for an intruder. Entering the pouring room at the back of the shop, she stopped short and caught her breath.

Shelving units had been tipped over, and many of the plaster molds had been smashed on the concrete floor. Surveying the area, Tammy surmised well over a hundred molds had been destroyed. Two of the three pouring tables had been dismantled and broken into small pieces. The only thing still in place were the two shelf units that were heavy wood and attached to the wall.

Tammy called the sheriff. He was at the hospital, half an hour away, but would get there as soon as possible. He was going to send one of his deputies to start the investigation. Not knowing if the shop would be closed for several days again, she didn't dare fire off the kiln.

She walked around to see if anything else was missing or destroyed. Not seeing anything else amiss, she dragged a chair from the main classroom to the front lobby to wait for the deputy. As she sat there, she wished it was Zeke who was well and answering the call. This latest sabotage would prevent her from getting back to the hospital as quickly as she wanted to.

A cruiser pulled in, and Deputy Phillip Becker exited the car. Tammy noticed how much he looked like his dad, the sheriff. Phillip was a senior when Tammy was a freshman. She hadn't known him in school, but she knew of him as he was involved in all the sports programs and was quite an athlete.

They even have the same walk.

"They broke in through a back window," Tammy said, joining him in the parking lot.

A second car pulled in. Deputy Collins, camera in hand, asked Becker where he wanted to start.

"Go with Tammy and get shots of the window where they broke in. I'll be inside looking around," Becker replied.

"Lead the way," Collins said.

Tammy stood back while he took the pictures.

"Did you walk near the window at all before we got here?"

"No, I stood just about where I am right now."

"Good to know. We have a clear set of sneaker prints in the dirt under the window," he said, recording the prints from several different angles. "Let's head inside. I'll print the window after I'm done taking pictures."

Becker was in the lobby checking out the register area.

"Did you happen to walk back here at all?" he asked Tammy.

"No, I saw the register hadn't been touched, so I moved on to the other rooms. Why?"

He held up a piece of paper with a gloved hand.

"Do you recognize this phone number?"

"I don't, but that's not to say my aunt wouldn't."

"True," he said, slipping it into an evidence bag.

"Collins, the room in the back has been ripped apart. We need pictures of everything."

"Right on it."

"When was the last time you were here?" Becker asked.

"I was here yesterday morning."

So, whoever did this did it in the late afternoon or last night."

"Someone's been really busy in the last twenty-four hours. First Zeke and now here. I'm beginning to wonder if it is worth it to keep the shop after all," Tammy said, sighing.

"Your aunt has put her everything into this shop for many years. The Idle Chat is a Braddock landmark. We'll get who did this and who has Clara."

"You sound just like your dad."

"Is that a bad thing?" he asked, smiling.

"No, it was meant as a compliment."

"Thank you. Now let's go see what Collins is up to."

"I got pictures of everything," he said as they entered the room. "It's sad, really. Some of the dates on these molds go back thirty years. They can never be replaced."

"My aunt has been collecting them since she opened the shop twenty-five years ago. The other day I was kidding with her she had way too many molds and now this. It's like I jinxed the place."

"I don't believe in jinxes," Sheriff Becker said, entering the room behind Tammy. "What a mess!"

"Yes, it is," she said. "I don't think many of the molds can be saved. This is going to take days to clean up."

"I'm afraid I have to agree with you," the sheriff said. "Maybe I can get some people together for a clean-up party. I'm sure there are many locals in the town who would jump in and help. After all, Clara has served as a selectman for twelve years and done many good things for the people here."

"That would be so awesome. I'm afraid I don't know or haven't reconnected with many people in Braddock since I've been back. Any help would be appreciated."

"I'm sure this will be covered by Clara's insurance, but I suggest you take your own pictures of the damage for your aunt's personal records," the sheriff advised. "We will fill out a report and give you a copy to use to file your aunt's claim."

"I'm going out to print the window," Collins said. "Sheriff, I did get pictures of well-defined sneaker prints left under the jimmied window. They look to be about men's, size eleven."

"Good. Let me know if the window can be locked or if it has been too damaged."

"I feel like I should be sleeping here to prevent anything else from happening. But if I sleep here, they may do something to my aunt's cabin. It's almost a no-win situation."

"You will not sleep here alone. As much as I love Clara and the Idle Chat, I know she would agree with me that no business is worth anyone's life. At least at the cabin, you have Clara's homemade security system installed to protect you."

"I wish you had given me that bit of advice before they took my aunt. Maybe I would have caved and not argued with her to keep the shop."

"You had no way of knowing what would unfold."

"Did you see Zeke at the hospital?"

"I didn't go to ICU, but I did talk to Paul. He doesn't look for any change within twenty-four hours, maybe more. I'm on my way to talk to Toby Brown about several matters, as I couldn't find him earlier today. Then I am off to the airport to pick up Zeke's parents and bring them to see their son."

"Sheriff, the locking mechanism has been popped right out of the wooden frame of the window and can't be locked. Do you want me to find something to block off the window?" Collins asked.

"There's some wood piled up on the far side of the building my aunt uses for tabletops during Braddock in Bloom. I don't know if you can find anything there to use," Tammy said.

"I have to say, in all the years I have known Wilmont Sawyer, I have never seen him wear sneakers. And I don't think his feet are big enough to be size eleven," the sheriff said. "Not that I'm making any kind of excuse for Sawyer. I'm just stating my observations of the past."

"I don't know if Wilmont Sawyer could even get his physique through the window. Why would he even do this if he has moved on and bought property elsewhere?" Tammy replied.

"What do you mean he bought property somewhere else?' the sheriff asked. "How do you know that?"

"He told me when I went to get the list of properties he owns under other names. The list I handed over to you. He showed me paperwork for a large amount of acreage he bought on the edge of town to build his condo development."

"You didn't mention he said he gave up on this area. So, the scale of guilt is leaning more and more to Toby Brown."

"I would say yes. The way he is harassing Hattie Cotton every day, it appears he has no intention of giving up until he gets all the properties he wants."

"Phillip, you have things under control here?"

"Yeah, we're almost done. As soon as Collins secures the window and I print the busted pouring tables, we'll be returning to the station."

"Good. I'm heading to Flashpoint Realty and then to Sawyer Realty. Tammy, I'll see you at the hospital later on today."

"I'm stopping at the hardware store to order a new set of keys for Aunt Clara. I only received two from the locksmith and I know my aunt likes to have at least three. I want to get her the peacock keys she likes so much so things will be back to the way they were before all this happened. I will be heading to see Zeke right after that."

Tammy sat in the front lobby, waiting for the deputies to finish up what they were doing so she could lock up after they left. It wasn't long before they completed their work and were gone. She returned to the pouring room and surveyed the area.

My aunt doesn't deserve this. Whoever did this doesn't have a heart or any regard for another human being.

She kicked one of the molds out of frustration. When she did, a flash of light caught her eye. Looking closer, she spotted a coin buried in the dust of the broken molds. Reaching for it, she stopped herself an inch away from picking it up. She blew the dust off the surface and revealed a twenty-dollar gold piece.

This isn't mine, and it wasn't here yesterday when I left. The coin has to belong to whoever broke in and destroyed the place.

She called the police station and asked them to send back one of the deputies to pick it up.

Maybe they'll get a fingerprint off the coin. This is an expensive, lucky piece to lose.

"Tammy!"

"Back here in the pouring room," she answered.

"Dispatch says you found something we need to see," Collins said, fully gloved and holding an evidence bag.

"A coin, an expensive coin," she answered, pointing to the spot where it lay.

"Are you sure it's not your aunt's?"

"I'm almost positive. It wasn't here yesterday."

"Okay. We'll take it in for processing, he said, picking it up and dropping it in the clear bag. "Someone's going to be extremely upset they lost this. Don't mention you found the coin to anyone, okay?"

"I won't say a word," she promised.

They walked out together to the parking lot. Collins waited until Tammy locked the front door and was safely in her car. He waved, got in his cruiser, and drove away.

Now, onto the hardware store.

Stan Perry, the owner of the hardware store, was standing behind the counter when Tammy arrived. He was sorting key blanks and hanging them on the corresponding hooks.

"Just the man I wanted to see," she said, walking up to the counter.

"What can I do for you today?"

"Do you remember the peacock keys you made for my aunt?"

Yes, I do. She loves those keys. Why do you ask?"

"I had to have the locks changed at Idle Chat. The locksmith gave me two keys, but I would like to get them turned into the same peacock keys my aunt had previously. I would also like four instead of two if that's possible."

"I can't do it today. Your aunt brought in a magazine that had a picture of the keys and wanted to know if I could get the blanks from the company I normally ordered from. I couldn't help her at the time but began to search and found a place that carried them. I only ordered three for your aunt and no others to sell."

"So, no one else in the area should have this specific key?"

"Not that I know of; at least they didn't get them from me. And I know Jason, the locksmith, doesn't carry them either. It was kind of like a special thing we provided just for Clara."

"Is it possible to order them again so the keys will be the same when my aunt is found?"

"I can, but it will take about a week for them to get here. If you leave me one of the keys, I will make them up when they come in and call you when they are ready," he offered.

"That would be great. Do you want me to pay you now?"

"No. Let's make sure I can get the blanks first."

"I'll look forward to hearing from you," Tammy said, handing him a key.

"Before you go, has there been any word on Clara?" Stan asked.

"Nothing yet, but the sheriff is working really hard to find her," she replied.

"My wife and I keep our eyes and ears open for any little information we can gather to help. The sheriff will find her. He's good at what he does, and he really cares for the people of this town. He won't give up until Clara is home safe and sound."

"Thank you, Stan. We'll find her; I know we will."

Tammy arrived at the hospital and checked in at the front desk. Zeke was in the ICU, and they gave her the directions to get there. Stepping off the elevator, she stopped at the nurse's station. They showed her to Zeke's room and told her she couldn't stay any more than five minutes.

He was in a private room, and Tammy found herself catching her breath when she opened the door. Zeke was hooked up to machines tracking his vitals, heartbeat, and brain waves. He looked like he was in a peaceful sleep. She moved a chair next to the bed and sat down. Holding his hand, she softly spoke to him.

"You hang in there. Your mom and dad are on their way here to see you. The sheriff would never admit it, being the tough guy he is, but he is worried sick about you, as am I."

She took a breath.

"I don't know if you can hear me or not, but I need you to know I had more than a crush on you in school. You were always spending time with Emily and the other cheerleaders, and I knew I didn't measure up to the popular group. So, I worshiped you from afar, as they say."

She shifted in her chair and reached over to brush his bangs away from his face. A single tear slid down her cheek.

"I just found you again after all these years apart. Don't you dare slip away from me again. We will have a future together, and I will never give up on you or the belief you will recover from this completely," she said, squeezing his hand.

"It's time for you to leave," the nurse said, poking her head in the door.

"I'll be right out. Zeke, I'll be downstairs in the waiting room. I'm not going to leave the hospital until I know you are okay. You rest and fight this with everything you got."

She leaned over and kissed his forehead before she left the room. The nurse at the station told her she could return for five minutes each hour. Tammy thanked her and returned to the waiting room in the lobby. Taking out her laptop, she opened her work-in-process and started to type. Her thoughts kept drifting to Zeke upstairs, but she fought through it to concentrate on her words.

Here I was thinking I was returning to a boring little town, and I would have half a book written by now. Stick with it, girlfriend, or you will be returning to the city out of necessity.

Tammy had been writing for a while when she checked her watch to see if she could return for another visit with Zeke. She made sure her work was saved and shut down the computer.

While waiting for the elevator, she heard her name being called. Turning around, she saw the sheriff and two other people heading her way. She knew they were Zeke's parents even though she hadn't seen them in years, as Zeke was the spitting image of his dad.

"Tammy, I think you know Maggie and Will Peters," the sheriff said.

"It's been a long time since we've seen you," Maggie said. "I think you were still in high school."

"I was in the gang," Tammy said, smiling.

"And now you are seeing our Zeke," Will said. "Imagine that."

"We've only been out on one date. I was just going up to see him, but I will stay down here so you can go see your son. You can only stay five minutes at a time, and the ICU is strict about how many people can visit at once. I'll be in the waiting room when you return."

"I'm going up with Maggie and Will but will stay at the nurse's station. We'll return shortly," the sheriff said, stepping into the elevator.

Tammy set the computer next to the chair knowing they would return fairly quickly, and it would be a waste of time to even open her document. She stared at the television, waiting for the time to pass. Her stomach growled, and she realized she hadn't eaten all day. Even though the vending machine coffee was terrible, it would give her something in her stomach until she could get something to eat.

Sheriff Becker returned and sat down next to her. He was silent as he sat there, head bowed.

"I never thought I would see one of my deputies in the hospital and so helpless. Not in this town anyway," he said in a whisper. "It's so hard to see him like that."

"He's going to be fine. You keep telling me to stay positive; now it's my turn to say it to you. Did you talk to Toby Brown today?"

"I did. And he was out of town at a real estate seminar in Portland. He left at six in the morning and didn't return until after midnight. I called the hotel and verified he was there. I spoke to the gentleman who ran the course, and he said Brown was there for the whole program."

"So, if it wasn't Brown, it had to be his so-called partner. Or...Wilmont Sawyer," Tammy finished. "Who did Zeke see right before he got clobbered?"

"I don't know, but it's time to push for the identity of his silent partner. Do you think if you sat with a police sketch artist, you could give us a composite of the man you saw eating with Brown at the diner?"

"I didn't see his facial features well enough. He pulled his ballcap down over his face as he ran."

"Too bad."

"Here comes Zeke's parents."

"My son is resting. The doctor assured us he will come out of this fine.

He said the swelling has already started to go down, and Zeke is strong and in good health. He promised to call us with any change. The ICU is closed in the evening for visitors. Tammy, the nurse, said you could come back at eight tomorrow morning."

Tammy's stomach growled.

"I'm so sorry. I haven't eaten a thing today, and my stomach is reminding me of that fact."

"We haven't eaten since we left Florida this morning. How about you give us a ride to Zeke's house, and we stop somewhere on the way there for a late-night supper?" Will suggested. "Unless, of course, you have other plans already."

"No, I don't, and I would love to have supper with you. Shall we go?"

"Tammy, I will check in with you tomorrow," the sheriff said. "Maggie, Will, good to see you again."

"You too, Harry. Make sure you catch whoever did this to our boy," Maggie said.

"I promise. We'll catch them, and they'll go away for a very long time."

"Good. Let's get something to eat. Zeke is in good hands here," Maggie said, hooking her arm in Tammy's. "Lead the way."

They ended up at The Brown Bear Café. Tammy could see where Zeke got his love for Reuben sandwiches as his father didn't even open the menu and knew what he wanted. She caught his parents up on her family and her own life since she left Braddock. They, in turn, told her about Zeke's breakup with Emily and how much it had destroyed their son. Upset to hear about Clara when they landed, they hoped she would be found soon.

Maggie admitted to Tammy the sheriff assured them their son had recovered from the fiancé fiasco and was extremely happy to be dating her. This gave both of his parents a lighter heart, knowing Zeke had moved on with his life.

Tammy dropped them off at their son's house with the promise to return in the morning to take Will to the local car rental place. Zeke's truck was still in police impound, so they had nothing to drive to and from the hospital. She offered the use of her aunt's car which was sitting in the driveway, but they politely refused. She returned to the cabin and checked the answering machine, but it wasn't flashing.

Chapter Twelve

Sheriff Becker texted Tammy while she was drinking her morning coffee. He had assembled a cleaning party for the pouring room and needed her to be at Idle Chat at three in the afternoon to let everyone in.

This is the town I expected to return to.

At nine o'clock, she was sitting in Zeke's driveway, waiting for his parents to come out. She had to be at the shop at three, so she had five hours to do what she needed to do. First, she would run to the hospital and see Zeke before his parents arrived for the day, then she was going to talk to Wilmont Sawyer. The sheriff had already been there, but Tammy knew Sawyer trusted her more than he did the law and might open up to where he had been when Zeke was attacked.

Tammy dropped Maggie and Will off at the car rental shop and promised to see them later at the hospital. She stopped at the nurse's station upon her arrival at the ICU. They told her there was no change in Zeke's condition. The chair was still in the room from her previous visit, and she pulled it up closer to the head of the bed.

She stroked his cheek while telling him everything was going to be all right.

"I need to see those beautiful green eyes open."

She paused and took a deep breath, not wanting to cry again in front of Zeke, whether he could see her or not.

"While you've been here, someone broke into Idle Chat and smashed a huge number of Aunt Clara's molds to smithereens. The pouring room is a total disaster. The town's locals are coming together to clean up the shop this afternoon."

Tammy stood up to leave.

"I'll be back later. Your mom and dad should be here shortly. The Doc says the swelling is going down in that hard head of yours. Please stay strong. I can't see my future without you in it, Mr. Peters."

She waved to the nurses on the way to the elevator.

First stop, Sawyer Realty.

Pulling into a parking spot right in front of the realty office, Tammy noticed the place was in total darkness. She walked up to the front window, shielded her eyes from the sunlight, and peered in. The overhead lights were out, and there was no movement. Trying the door next, she found it locked.

Where are you, Mr. Sawyer?

Taking out one of her business cards, she wrote the words call me on the back and slipped it through the mail slot on the front door. Knowing Zeke's parents were probably at the hospital at this point, she put the car in gear and headed for home to do some writing before going to the ceramic shop.

The sheriff sent her a message saying they had lifted a partial thumbprint off the coin she found. They were running it through AFIS as they spoke but there were no hits as of yet. She wrote for another two hours, made a turkey sandwich to go, and left for the ceramic shop.

The road the shop sat on was packed with cars, including the parking lot behind the shop.

There's still an hour to go before anyone should be here to clean. What is going on?

Tammy managed to squeeze her car into a spot up against the back of the building. She locked the car and walked to Hattie's house to see if they knew what was happening on the street. Before she got too far, she realized people were going in and out of the old Grady mansion next to the Cotton house and this was the reason for all the cars. Knowing there was a chance she might run into Toby Brown she entered the house anyway.

People were walking around with items from the house in their hands. Each item had an orange price sticker on it. Putting two and two together, she surmised Brown was holding an estate sale to empty the house of the less expensive contents he hadn't already sold.

Tammy walked around perusing the items still left for sale. She picked up an old hurricane lamp and looked it over. The globe was a deep, ruby-red color, and the base was formed out of hammered pewter. In the near future, she would be buying her own house in Braddock and would like this in her writing room.

"What are you doing here?" Brown yelled, startling everyone in the room and almost causing her to drop the lamp.

"This is a public estate sale, is it not?" Tammy replied, keeping her cool even though everyone was staring at her.

"This is my property, and I don't want you here."

"Fine, I'll take my money elsewhere," she said, returning the lamp to its spot where she got it from.

"Are you really here to buy stuff or are you just being your normal nosy self?"

"I was here to shop," she insisted. "I will be buying a house in the near future, or have you forgotten already?"

"Fine, the more of this garbage I don't have to tow to the dump the better. Don't cause any trouble or I will personally throw you out the front door myself. Understand?"

"You and what army?" Tammy asked, causing the people around them to chuckle.

"I'll be keeping my eye on you," Brown threatened, limping away.

"Whatever," she said, picking up the lamp again and walking into the next room.

Tammy wandered around the house, and after being inside, she now understood why it was considered a mansion. Standing and admiring the double staircase leading upstairs, she couldn't believe Brown was going to tear this grand old place down and replace it with cookie-cutter houses. She was sad thinking Braddock would lose another piece of its history.

"This house was built in 1836 by Colonel Jedidiah Blackstone," a voice said.

Sylvia Bagley, the town historian was standing behind her. She was holding several old books and an old map that had been hanging on the wall in the last room Tammy had just walked through. Sylvia and her Aunt Clara were good friends and had been for a very long time. They used to exchange stories about historical events over tea as she was growing up. Fascinated, she would sit next to her aunt for hours listening to the two women.

"Mrs. Bagley, it's so nice to see you again. I'd give you a hug, but both our hands are full," Tammy said. "I had no idea this house was so old."

"It's one of the oldest in Braddock. I desperately tried to talk Mr. Brown into turning the house over to the Historical Society, but he refused. The only way he would is if we bought it at three times more than what he paid for it. He knows the property appraised at three hundred and sixty thousand. He also knew we didn't have that kind of money and it would be impossible for us to raise it in the time frame he gave us."

"What were you going to use the house for?"

"That wasn't the point. The point was to keep it from being torn down and losing its historical value to the town. We would have eventually found someone to buy the house who wouldn't have destroyed it but restored it to it's beautiful state. Do you know it is rumored the colonel used this house as a stop on the Underground Railroad?"

"Can't the town put the mansion under protection by adding it to the historical register?"

"We tried that avenue. Unfortunately, we could not find any proof it was actually used for that purpose. And Brown's attorney was quick to pick up on the fact we couldn't."

"This is so sad. You would figure where he was a Civil War colonel, they would save the mansion for that reason alone."

"Not enough of a reason, I'm afraid. And to make matters worse, Toby Brown's mother is on the approval committee, so you know she's not going to stand in her son's way of becoming successful."

"Now it makes more sense why the request was turned down," Tammy replied.

"You should go upstairs and check out the bedrooms. They knew what luxury was back then. The moldings are to die for, and the tins ceilings are something you don't see anymore."

"If you don't mind my asking, what did Brown buy the place for?"

"He got it through a bank auction to pay off back taxes. His winning bid was for the measly amount of one hundred and ten thousand. The purchase included all the surrounding land which we wanted to search for any tunnels using ground penetrating radar."

"I'm moving back here permanently. I would love to live in and restore this gorgeous mansion. I want you to go back to Brown and offer him three hundred and seventy-five thousand for the house. That's way over his asking price. Let's see if he is serious about selling the place. If he asks where you got the money tell him you applied for and received an emergency grant to purchase the mansion. Don't let him know I am the one who will be fronting the money, or he will refuse because it's me."

"Are you serious?"

"I am. Now go before he sees you talking to me. I will be at Idle Chat later if he gives you an answer. I am going upstairs to see what I may be purchasing."

Upstairs, the rooms were overly large and exquisite, just as Sylvia described. The tin ceilings were badly in need of a paint job, and the wallpaper was peeling off almost everywhere. Tammy knew by looking at the thickness of the paint peelings on the floor that it was lead-based and the whole place would have to be stripped and treated.

The biggest room had decorative French doors, which opened to a stately balcony overlooking the backyard. This room is the one she would claim for her own bedroom. A full-sized fireplace, built of neutral-colored flagstones, provided heat back in the day. She looked around for any clue of a modern-day heating system and saw old-fashioned, standup iron radiators that had been hidden under falling wallpaper.

Her stomach was doing flip-flops just thinking about the possibilities becoming realities if Brown would sell. Tammy knew the restoration would be costly, but it would be so worth it in the end.

She walked to the fireplace to get a closer look at its condition. Tammy wiggled a few of the individual stones to see how loose they were. As she pulled on one that was sticking out further than the others at the base of the hearth it fell out into her hand. She knelt down on all fours to look inside the hole.

"What are you doing?" a voice demanded from behind her.

Luckily, she was in front of the hole, and she quickly sat down to cover up what she was doing. Grabbing the lamp, she peeled off the orange sticker and held it up for Brown to see.

"This fell off the lamp and I was searching for it on the floor. I didn't want to go to the cashier and not have a price on my item and hold up the line," Tammy said.

"Are you almost done up here?"

"Almost. I have two more rooms to look through. I found the most beautiful hand-made doilies for Aunt Clara," she said, holding one of them up.

"I don't know what you're up to, but I don't like it. You got five more minutes, and then you're out of here. Got it?"

"Got it. For a person who wants to clear the house out, you sure have a funny way of showing it."

"Just get a move on," he growled, walking out the door.

She sat there folding the doilies into a neat pile in case he was watching her from the hallway. Confident he was gone, she pulled out her keys and turned on the mini flashlight hanging from them. The beam caught a flash of something shiny in the hole. Reaching in, she pulled out a handful of gold coins. Gold coins which were identical to the one dropped in the Idle Chat.

"Are you done up there?" Brown yelled.

Tammy quickly stuffed the coins in her purse, replaced the stone, and moved swiftly to the French doors. Not a second later, Brown entered the room and stood there glaring at her.

"You haven't even left the room," he said suspiciously.

"I was looking out the doors at the balcony. It's huge."

"Who cares about some stupid balcony? Downstairs, NOW!"

"What is your problem? Have you got something to hide up here?" she challenged him.

"Why you uppity… I ought to…"

"Ought to what, Mr. Brown?" the sheriff asked, standing in the doorway.

"Nothing," he stammered, rushing past the sheriff and down the stairs.

"You sure know how to push his buttons," the sheriff said. "And I see he is still limping."

"Wait until you see what I found," Tammy said. "And what I found out."

"One of these days, no one is going to be around to run interference for you," he warned.

They returned to the downstairs under the watchful eye of Toby Brown. Tammy paid for her finds and walked to the ceramic shop with the sheriff and his wife, Shirley. It was a few minutes before three, and a crowd of about thirty people had gathered at the door of the ceramic shop. A tall stack of trash barrels, shovels, and work gloves were at the ready to use.

"Let's get this door open and get to work," Stan Perry said. "I brought all the supplies we need from the hardware store to get the job done. Donny from Braddock Disposal will be by in the morning to empty the barrels."

"I can't believe this; how do I thank you all?" Tammy said.

"You don't. This is the way our town used to be prior to all this real estate rubbish that has torn it apart. We all love Clara and will do whatever needs to be done to help her," Shirley said. "Your aunt and I went to school together. She has always been there for me, and I will always be there for her. That's the way it works around here."

Tammy unlocked the door and went around to open the loading dock. It would be easier to drag the barrels out there instead of going all the way through the shop. While the woman shoveled the broken molds into the barrels, some of the men went to work rebuilding the shelves. On one of his trips dragging a full barrel to the outside, the sheriff reminded her as he went by she had something to show him. She whispered it would have to wait until later when no one else was around.

Tammy ordered pizzas, bottles of soda, and water to be delivered at six o'clock to feed the crew. They ate in shifts, so there was always someone working.

By eight o'clock, the last of the dust was being swept up, and all the shelves had been replaced. If you had seen the pouring room and the number of molds there before the break-in, the only visible difference now was the empty shelves that once housed the piles of molds.

"I don't know how to thank you all. This would have taken me days to clean up," Tammy said, looking around.

"We did this for Clara," Stan said. "Now, I don't know about anyone else, but I'm going home to take a nice long, hot shower."

"Same here," echoed around the group.

Tammy stood by the door and personally thanked each individual as they left. The only one waiting around was the sheriff. She locked the front door and waved the sheriff over to the register counter. She reached for her purse and rummaged around in the bottom of it.

"Do these look familiar to you?" she asked, setting the gold coins on the counter she found in the hidden compartment in the fireplace.

"Yeah, real familiar. I did some research on the one you turned in. These are California Gold Tokens. They are actually considered to be ingots and not coins at all. These are all dated the same year, 1852. Where did you get them?"

"I was walking around upstairs at the old Grady mansion. There was a flagstone sticking out in the fireplace in the first bedroom to the right. I moved the stone, and these were hidden behind it."

"You took them from the house? You do realize these belong to Toby Brown as they were on his property?"

"I know that. But what if he had found others in the house, and he was the one who dropped the coin while he was vandalizing my aunt's shop? I had to keep these for proof. The one found here might have come from the Grady place."

"Again, we can't tie him and the coins together without any definite proof."

"I know, but he intends to tear the house down, and these would have probably been discarded in the rubble."

"That doesn't mean you should have removed them from the property."

"Well, I did, and for a good reason. Proof."

"Do me a favor. Hold onto these and don't tell a soul you have them or where they came from, not even Zeke. I plan on taking the coin I have out in front of Brown to see what kind of reaction I get. I don't want anyone to know there are others like it."

"I will put them in my aunt's safe."

"Sylvia Bagby tells me you and her are in cahoots to purchase the Grady mansion. I don't know if he'll cave for a mere three hundred and seventy-five thousand when he can build a multiple of houses and make a whole lot more money."

Yes, but he still needs to purchase Hattie Cotton's place and the Idle Chat. I told Sylvia to suggest to him that all the money from the sale could buy a lot of acreage elsewhere in the town, which he wouldn't have to fight so hard to buy. If he is any kind of businessman, he would figure out selling the Grady house at a triple profit and not having to spend another half million or so for the adjoining properties would be a better use of his money. Not that it's his money anyway."

"The place needs a lot of work."

"I know, but it doesn't have to be done all at once. Can you imagine how beautiful it will be when it's restored? I can see myself living there and running writer's retreats there."

"Did you make the offer to purchase it before or after you found the gold coins?"

"Before. You knew I was going to start looking for a house of my own, and I could work on restoring it while I write. If only Brown would give it up."

"I wouldn't hold my breath. He doesn't care about historical importance at all, only money."

"I'm prepared to go a little higher if need be," Tammy stated. "Sylvia and her group want to do ground penetrating radar in the backyard to see if they can find any proof of the tunnels tied to the Underground Railroad. Brown hasn't let them on the property because if they find even one tunnel, they could request the house be put on the historic register, and the mansion couldn't be torn down even with Brown's mother running interference. It would be so cool to live in a place which has been a huge part of our country's history."

"Good luck. I'll keep my fingers crossed for you. I need to get home. Five-thirty comes awful early in the morning."

"Before you go, did you stop to see Zeke this afternoon? I was there early this morning but didn't make it back there today."

"Doc says the swelling is continuing to subside, but he hasn't come to yet."

"I'm going there first thing in the morning before his parents get there for the day."

"The nurses set up the empty room adjacent to Zeke's for Maggie and Will so they can stay the day and be near their son."

"That's awesome. Have a good night and I'm sure I'll run into you tomorrow, somewhere."

"Lock up and head home yourself. I don't want you hanging around here alone at night," the sheriff said, opening the door.

"I'll be right behind you. I'm going to make sure all the doors and windows are secure, and then I'm gone," she promised.

She stayed in the shower longer than usual. The remains of the destruction at Idle Chat disappeared down the drain with the lavender body wash and the hot, steamy water. Bundled in the new fluffy robe and slippers she had bought after the fire at her cottage, she sat at the kitchen island with a cup of tea and made a list of everything she wanted to get done the following day.

Lying in bed, she found her imagination running wild with ideas of how she could renovate the Grady mansion. She knew it was a long shot she would get the place, but it was fun to imagine herself living there. If she did have the chance to buy it, she would have to reconsider purchasing the ceramic shop at the same time. Then again, if they could figure out who was causing all the problems in Braddock, she might not have to buy the ceramic shop.

At ten o'clock, Tammy was riding the elevator to the ICU. She stepped off and saw Maggie talking to the nurses at the desk. She approached the desk, and Zeke's mother turned. She had tears in her eyes and pulled Tammy in for a big hug.

"He's awake. He's talking to the sheriff right this moment, but he was asking for you," Maggie said, letting her go.

"What wonderful news. I can't wait to see him.," Tammy said, tearing up herself.

"This afternoon, they will be moving him out of ICU to a private room where anyone can visit with him and stay as long as they like. The doctor wants him to stay a couple more days for rest and further observation."

"You must be so relieved," Tammy said, taking hold of Maggie's hand.

"I am. Will went home to change and shower because he spent the night here last night. He doesn't know Zeke is awake. I was going to call him and tell him, but his son wanted to surprise him when he got back."

"How long has the sheriff been with him?"

"About twenty minutes. He's trying to get any information he can to find out who attacked my Zeke. He also told me he processed the paperwork for Zeke to take ten days off and it won't be using up his sick pay."

"When he woke up, he kept repeating the word blinky, and we couldn't figure out what he was trying to say."

"Blinky is his black lab," Tammy said. "The sheriff has been watching the dog at his house."

"We found out he was talking about his dog when he became a little more coherent," the nurse said. "The sheriff was going to tell Zeke that Blinky was at his house to ease his worrying about the dog."

"Does the doctor think there will be any lasting effects from his injury?"

"None. The doctor gave us nothing but good news this morning. We have open end tickets for our return trip, so we will be staying with Zeke for another week. I want to make sure he is well on the road to complete recovery before we leave. He's supposed to be coming down to Florida to spend Thanksgiving with us, but we won't see him again until then."

"That will be nice for all of you."

"He loves our pool and spends most of his days floating around with a beer in hand. Have you ever been to Florida?"

"Just once. I was doing a book signing in Tampa and was only there for one day. I didn't have time to see any of the local sites."

"Well, maybe you can discuss it with Zeke and come spend the holiday with us, too."

The sheriff exited Zeke's room and didn't look happy. He joined the group of chatting women.

"How is he?" Tammy asked.

"He's good but tired. He did want to know if his dad was back yet, and he also asked if you were out here."

"Does he know who hit him?" Tammy asked.

"No, he was hit from behind and never saw his assailant."

"Does he remember seeing anyone or anything right before he got hit?"

"So many questions," Maggie said.

"He didn't see anything which should have caused him to get hit. At least he didn't think he did. Zeke said he had just come out of the mall, put the gifts he had bought on the front seat and bam, he got hit."

"So, someone thinks he saw something. Did he say how he got away?"

"After he blacked out, the next thing he remembered was waking up in some kind of tool shed. His hands were duct-taped together. He said he fumbled around in the dark and found a set of hedge trimmers. He sawed the tape using the blades and managed to escape out of the shed through a small window."

"How did he end up at my aunt's cabin?"

"He thinks he was wandering around in the woods for a couple of hours, but he's not sure about the real amount of time that lapsed before he spotted the signpost at the end of Clara's road. He headed for the cabin, climbed up on the porch, and blacked out again."

"Why's everyone looking so serious?" Zeke's dad asked, stepping off the elevator. "Has something happened to my son?"

"Follow me," the nurse told him, winking at Maggie and Tammy.

She told Will to wait at the door, and she disappeared inside.

"Come in," she said, holding the door open so he could see his son.

Tammy could see Zeke sitting up in bed when the nurse stepped to the side.

"Hi, Dad," she heard him say as the door closed.

"He looks so much better already," Tammy said, fighting back more tears of happiness.

"I'm taking some of my deputies and going out to comb the woods for houses with a tool shed in the area of Clara's cabin. I don't think Zeke could have walked very far in his dazed condition."

"Good luck."

Tammy, Zeke wants to see you," Will said, exiting his son's room. "He's really tired so don't stay too long. Don't tell him I said so."

"Thank you, Mr. Peters."

"Will, please. Maggie, I told Zeke we were going to grab some lunch, and we'll be back after they move him to his new room. Ready?"

"I'll be on my way, too," the sheriff said, heading to the elevator with Zeke's parents.

"Is it okay if I go in?" Tammy asked the nurse.

"Sure, just make it short. He's already had a lot of visitors this morning."

Tammy opened the door and slipped inside. Zeke's eyes were closed, and she thought maybe he had dozed off, and she didn't want to wake him up. She opened the door to leave.

"I'm not asleep. Please don't go."

"Zeke, I was so worried about you," she said, taking his hand. "So was everyone."

"I don't know what happened or why I was targeted. It wasn't a robbery; the sheriff said they didn't steal anything from the truck."

"Someone thought you saw something even if you didn't, and they couldn't take any chances," she said. "All I can say is it's a good thing you have such a hard head."

"The only thing I regret about the whole thing is maybe if I had stayed in the shed, they would have eventually taken me to where Clara is being held."

"Or they could have killed you," Tammy added. "You were smart to get out of there. No matter how much I want my aunt to be found, I wouldn't have wanted you to put your life in jeopardy by waiting around."

"I know, but maybe—"

"Maybe nothing. Stop thinking about what you could have done and concentrate on getting better so we can spring you from this place."

"Doc says I can go home the day after tomorrow. He said the swelling should be totally gone by then, but I can't return to work for another week."

"Your mom said they were staying for another week before they return to Florida."

"I know. She thinks I'm still her little boy and need looking after. It's okay, though. I miss them when they're not around."

"A lot has happened in the last couple of days, but I'll wait until later to talk to you about it. Get some rest, and I'll see you after supper."

"Don't you be eating any Reubens without me," he said, smiling his old familiar smile.

"Too late," she said, giving him a kiss on the forehead.

He took both her hands.

"You can look into these green eyes any time you want to," he whispered.

Tammy knew instantly he had heard every word she said to him while he was in the coma.

Chapter Thirteen

After she left the hospital, Tammy drove to the ceramic shop and parked. There was still one more day of the estate sale at the Grady mansion. As she walked up the street, she looked around for Toby Brown's car and, not seeing it parked anywhere, she was a little more at ease about returning to the mansion to poke around some more.

"A return shopper," the lady behind the cash register said when she saw Tammy enter.

"Is Mr. Brown here today?"

"No, he had a meeting to attend to, so I am in charge. He's returning at five o'clock. Is there something I can help you with?"

"Thank you, but not really. Mr. Brown and I don't get along and I couldn't relax yesterday with him around."

"You're Clara's niece, aren't you? Between you and me, he doesn't seem to get along with anybody, especially the guy with the long hair."

"Long black hair?" Tammy asked.

"Yes, I believe it's black. The two times he's been here during the sale, it's been tucked up inside his ballcap."

"Has he been here today?"

"No. I heard him and Mr. Brown discussing a property they were going to buy in Fulton. He was going to check on it while Mr. Brown was at his meeting and report back to him later today."

"Do you know who this man is, his name, maybe?"

"No, he doesn't talk to anyone but Mr. Brown, and he hides his face like he doesn't want to be seen. He's kind of creepy. I have lived here my whole life and don't recognize him. Maybe if he got rid of some of the bushy facial hair, we could see who he is underneath."

"I never got to see the whole upstairs as Mr. Brown chased me out. I don't know what his problem is, but he sure can be spiteful. I guess he holds a grudge against me because my aunt won't sell to him."

"He does seem to be the type to hold a grudge," she agreed.

"I found the most beautiful doilies in the first bedroom yesterday. I was hoping there would be more linens in the other rooms," Tammy said, trying to make the woman think she was truly interested in shopping the sale.

"I don't know what's left up there, but you are welcome to look around."

"Thank you. Maybe I'll find a treasure everyone else has missed."

"You never know," she said, picking up a pile of receipts. "Have fun."

Tammy went into the first room and straight to the fireplace. She searched for any other loose or out-of-place stones but didn't find any. Next, she searched the mantel area. She ran her fingers over the rough wood hoping to find a notch or some other clue leading to another hidden compartment. Finding nothing, she moved on to the next bedroom.

Smaller in size than the first room, but still quite large, the crown molding was exquisite. Big chunks of the tin ceiling were lying on the floor, exposing a horsehair and slat ceiling underneath. The linen wallpaper was almost totally all on the floor like someone had ripped it off on purpose.

Searching for more coins, Mr. Brown?

She quickly perused the smaller fireplace in the room but found nothing. She did find an old, handwritten journal hidden under a piece of the fallen ceiling. She would ask how much the journal was and purchase it.

The third and fourth bedrooms were just about empty from the three-day sale. She did find a few more linens discarded on the floor. A broken mirror with an ornate gold frame was standing in the corner. Tammy picked it up to find it was extremely heavy. She knew she could replace the cracked mirror and took it with her thinking it would be nice to keep it in the house if she was able to purchase and restore the property.

"You found some treasures?" the clerk asked, watching Tammy place her items on and up against the counter.

"I believe I picked up what other people discarded. There are no prices on anything I have here. The book and the linens were strewn on the floor, and the broken mirror was sitting in the corner of the far room."

"The book wasn't part of the library contents, and these linens are random and not part of any sets I remember seeing while marking things. How about we say five dollars for the lot?"

"Really? That is so great," Tammy said, opening her purse to grab her wallet.

"Mr. Brown informed me anything left was going in a dumpster arriving tomorrow morning. Look around and see if there's anything else you want, and I will give you a good price. I'd rather someone take them home than have them end up in the Braddock landfill."

"In that case, I'll look around the first floor again. Would you hold my things behind your counter, please?"

"Done," she said, placing the mirror behind the counter.

Other customers had come in looking for last-minute buys. Tammy went the opposite way and entered the library. Rich-looking wooden bookcases surrounded her on three walls. The books had been picked through thoroughly. The ones left on the shelves were more modern and probably didn't belong to its earliest inhabitants.

This would make a phenomenal writing den.

The room had been designed with a male in mind. There were four indents on the wooden floor where a grand desk must have sat for many years. The fireplace had a leather mantel now disintegrating with age. A brass chandelier hung in the center of the room, extending downward from one of the most detailed tin ceilings Tammy had ever seen.

I wonder why no one wanted to take that chandelier down and buy it. It looks very old. The candle holders look like they are made of ruby glass.

"Obviously, Mr. Brown has no idea what he is doing, or he would have taken these tin ceilings down and sold them. This one has to be worth at least twelve to fifteen thousand. It's a shame they will be lost and never appreciated again," the clerk said, coming up behind her.

"It is a shame. The detail is outstanding. The crossed swords stamped into the tin panels lead me to believe this ceiling must have been installed for Colonel Blackstone himself. Do me a favor. Please don't tell Mr. Brown how much the ceilings might be worth. I have my reasons to keep that detail a secret."

"I know about your secret, and it's safe with me. I hope you get this old beauty."

"Sylvia?" Tammy asked.

"Yes, we were talking, and I told her how heartbroken I was at losing the old mansion. She told me about your secret and told me to keep my fingers crossed for your success in buying the place. I came to tell you it's almost five o'clock. If you want to escape before Mr. Brown arrives, you might want to skedaddle."

"There isn't much left to look through, so I'll grab my purchases and head out. Thank you for the warning."

Tammy was sitting in her car when she saw Brown's car turn onto the road. She ducked down, not wanting to be seen in the area. Waiting for him to pass where she was parked, her phone went off. She didn't recognize the number but answered it in case it was Zeke calling from the hospital.

"Hello, Tammy?"

"This is she. Who am I speaking to?"

"This is Sylvia Bagby. I just left a meeting with Mr. Brown. He said if we could raise our sale price to three hundred and ninety-five thousand, he would sell us the house."

"Why that price?"

"He said it has come to his attention another property for that amount has come up for sale. He can get all the land he needs for one price and not have to wait to purchase anything else before he could begin his housing development."

"That must have been the property his silent partner checked out in Fulton today," Tammy said, thinking out loud.

"Excuse me?"

"Oh, nothing. It's only twenty thousand more than I offered. I'm sure once I restore the house the value will more than triple. When do you have to get back to him?"

"I told him I would call him tonight as the house is due to be demolished the beginning of next week. If he doesn't call off the demolition at least five days before, he will lose his deposit on the equipment. So, what do you think?"

"I really want the house. Tell him you will pay the requested price, and the house will be sold to a trust held by the historical society. I will get in touch with my financial advisor and have him send a money transfer to my bank here. We can work out the details of how the property will be transferred to me after we make sure the first sale goes through."

"The whole town will thank you. You are saving a wonderful piece of our history."

"I'm not doing it just for the town. It's a grand old mansion, and I can't wait to live there," Tammy said honestly.

"I don't blame you one bit. If I had the money, I would buy it myself."

"You cannot breathe a word of this to anyone yet. The way gossip travels in this town, if word gets out, I am the one buying the house, he'll back out of the sale. This has to be kept totally secret," Tammy said, wondering how many other people Sylvia had already told.

"There will only be four of us involved. You, me, and the attorneys representing each party," Sylvia assured her.

"I hope so. I will get things started on my end and my attorney will be in touch with your attorney. Send me his information in an email that I can forward to mine."

"I am not trying to be pushy because you are already doing so much for the town, but will you allow us to search the grounds with radar to look for the tunnels?"

"Of course, the more history we can gather, the better. Let's get through the sales first," Tammy said.

"I'm going to call him right now and tell him we accept his offer. I hope he doesn't back out on us."

"Let me know what he says. He just passed me on the way to the mansion. The estate sale ended today, and if he's going to sell the mansion, maybe he'll leave the rest of the household items in there instead of spending the money on a dumpster to empty it. Tell him we'll take it as is. I'm afraid he will throw out the tin ceiling panels that have fallen and other things I want to restore."

"Okay. I'll tell him as is. I'll call you back shortly," Sylvia promised.

Butterflies danced in Tammy's stomach. Purchasing this house would cement her staying in Braddock. The idea of hosting other authors to a writing retreat at such a magnificent home was an exciting thought. Now that she had committed to this purchase, she had to have her advisor look over her finances to see if she could afford to buy Idle Chat at the same time.

Tammy drove to the Braddock Diner in the middle of town. She hadn't eaten there in years and wanted something different than the Brown Bear Café food. Asking for a booth in the back, she had brought her computer with her to do some writing while she ate. The waitress took her order for swordfish in a butter and lemon sauce. Sides of sweet potato French fries, summer squash, and a large root beer completed her order.

Opening her emails, she saw Sylvia had sent the requested information. Her agent had also messaged her, twice. He said he hoped she was doing well and wanted her to know her publisher was looking to firm up a deadline for a completed manuscript before the end of the current year. She didn't answer him back.

Only a quarter of the way through the new book, and Aunt Clara still missing, she was having a hard time wrapping her mind around a deadline date. There was no question about it; she had to force herself to sit down and write more than she was. This was her job, the way she earned her living. If she could only find her aunt things could return to normal, and she could adhere to a set schedule of writing.

"You look lost in thought," the waitress said, setting down her drink and house salad.

"I was."

"Don't you worry. The sheriff will find Clara."

"You know who I am," Tammy asked.

"Of course, I do. You're Tammy Wright, the author. I have seen your picture on the back of your books, and I have read everything you have released."

"Don't tell me. My aunt made you read them," Tammy said, smiling.

"No, my daughter did," she said, chuckling as she walked away.

Her salad was gone in no time. She didn't know how hungry she was until the food was set down in front of her. The waitress returned with her main course and took away the empty salad bowl. Looking at the slab of swordfish in front of her and smelling the wonderful aroma it was giving off, she closed her computer and gave her delicious dinner her full attention. In the middle of eating, her phone rang. Sylvia Bagby called to inform her Toby Brown had accepted the offer to sell as is. Butterflies danced in Tammy's stomach and her heart beat a little faster upon hearing the good news.

Tammy told her the two attorneys would handle it from here on, and she would forward the society's attorney information to her own as soon as she was off the phone. Sylvia thanked Tammy at least three more times before she hung up.

Wait until Zeke finds out I am buying a house. The Grady mansion, no less. He's going to freak and so will Aunt Clara.

She finished every morsel of her meal but passed on dessert. Checking her watch, she saw that there was only an hour before visiting hours were closed for the day, and if she wanted to see Zeke, she had to get a move on. Arriving at the hospital with half an hour to spare she stopped at the front desk to find out Zeke's new room number.

His parents were outside the room having a discussion with Doctor Downey. Tammy joined the group to see what was happening.

"Doc says Zeke can go home tomorrow, but only if he promises to take it easy and no driving for at least a few more days," Maggie said, squeezing Tammy's hand. "And I will be right there to make sure he follows the doctor's orders."

"He'll be happy to be going home. And I know Blinky will be glad to see him."

"Sheriff Becker said he would bring the dog over tomorrow night after supper," Will added.

"Not to be rude, but I'm going in and see Zeke before visiting hours close,"

152

Tammy said, reaching for the door.

"Tell him we'll see him in the morning," Will said.

"Well, look at you, sitting up and watching television," Tammy teased, walking up to the side of the bed.

"I know. And check out my stylish attire," he said, pulling on the top of his hospital gown.

"Classy. It shows a little too much leg, though."

"And a lot of other things if you're not careful," he said, chuckling.

"It's nice to see you have your sense of humor back."

"Doc says I can go home tomorrow."

"Your mom told me. That's wonderful news. Speaking of wonderful news, I have something exciting to tell you, but you can't breathe a word of it to anyone."

"You hit the lottery!"

"I wish, but no. Something better. I bought a house, or I am in the process of buying a house. Actually, it's a mansion."

"Excuse me?"

"I'm purchasing the old Grady mansion from Toby Brown, except he doesn't know it's me who is actually buying it," she gushed. "He thinks it's the historical society."

"Whoa! Back up and tell me the whole story from the beginning."

She explained while attending the estate sale, she ran into Sylvia Bagby, and things blossomed from there. Tammy ended her story by insisting Zeke keep everything a secret and not even tell his parents.

"Does that mean you will be staying here permanently?"

"Looks like it."

"You don't know how happy that makes me," he said, closing his eyes.

"It's almost eight o'clock. Tomorrow, I'm going to spend the day writing, but I will stop by your house after supper to check on you."

"I am tired. It's been a long day," he mumbled.

"Get some sleep," she said, pulling up his blankets and then quietly slipping out of the room.

Grabbing a wine cooler out of the refrigerator, Tammy took it out to the front porch and got comfortable in one of the rockers. It was eerily quiet for that time of night. The crickets weren't chirping, and the croaking of the tree frogs were subdued.

Twenty minutes later, Tammy understood why. A large dark cloud rolled in over the treetops from the west. The rain started out as a light drizzle but turned into a torrential downpour mixed with streaks of lighting and claps of thunder so loud the cabin shook from the vibrations. Her skin tingled from the electricity in the air. Moving her rocker, a little further back on the porch out of the reach of the rain, she watched the storm with fascination.

Living in the city with all its lights and tall buildings, she would never have been able to witness the power of Mother Nature the way she was seeing it now. An extremely bright flash lit up the sky like it was daytime. It was quickly followed by a clap of thunder, so ear-shattering Tammy knew something close by had to have been struck by the lighting.

This is getting a little too close for comfort. It's time to go inside.

Tammy locked the door and snagged another wine cooler. She sat in her aunt's recliner with one small light on next to her. Minutes later, the light flickered and went out.

Great, no electricity means no internet and no writing.

She sat in the dark, watching the storm through the windows of the cabin. It was obvious the electricity wouldn't be coming on any time soon, so she went to bed, hoping to get an early start to her writing the following day. Thinking of her aunt, she hoped she was somewhere safe, out of the reach of the storm.

The electricity was back on the next morning. She walked her aunt's property making sure there was no storm damage from the winds of the previous night while she drank her morning pick-me-up. Small branches littered the area, but nothing more. The rain had turned the pile of rubble that once was the cottage into even more of a mess than it had been previously.

Tammy returned to the cabin with the intention of calling a clean-up crew to come remove the debris but put it off until she could research who was in the area and how much it would cost. She was hoping her aunt's insurance would pay for the clean-up.

Pouring a second cup of coffee, she stared out the kitchen window, running details through her mind, hoping she would stumble upon something she had overlooked, which would tell her where her aunt was and who had her, but she came up with nothing new.

Deep into the words she was putting down on her computer, the morning turned into the afternoon without the author even noticing. She only looked up when her cell phone went off. Zeke was touching base to tell her he was home and was looking forward to seeing her later. His mother suggested Tammy come for supper, and she accepted, saying she would be there at five.

It was only two o'clock, and she was hungry. Rummaging through the kitchen cabinets, she found some saltine crackers. Cutting some thin slices off a block of cheddar cheese, she put them together, making herself a light snack to hold her over until supper. Tammy thought about calling the sheriff to see if there was any news on her aunt but decided not to, as she would see him later in the day.

At four-thirty, she shut down her computer, pleased with the tally of words she had completed for the day. Changing from her sweats to a new pair of jeans and a summer sweater, she left for Zeke's house.

A car pulled into the driveway as Tammy was exiting her car. Blinky was jumping around in the front seat and leaving nose prints on all the windows. The sheriff opened the door, and the lab jumped over him and out of the vehicle before he could react. Tammy called the dog, and he went right to her, so she was able to grab the leash.

"Blinky!" Zeke yelled from the front door.

The dog, recognizing Zeke's voice strained at the leash to get to him. Tammy let it go, and Blinky took off. He jumped up, danced around, and covered Zeke with wet, sloppy kisses. His owner was laughing and enjoying every minute of their reunion.

"You'd think they hadn't seen each other for years," Tammy said.

"It's great, isn't it?" the sheriff replied. "My dogs act the same way when the wife and I are gone for just a few hours."

"I'm more of a cat person, but I do love dogs, too."

"Hello, Sheriff. I want to thank you for taking care of Blinky while I was in the hospital. If you and Shirley ever go on vacation, let me know, and I'll take the dogs for you while you are gone."

"Thanks, we may take you up on your offer this Fall."

"So, anything new on the case?" Zeke asked.

"We checked with all the surrounding shop owners at the mall where you were parked. No one saw anything. The outside cameras covering the parking lot area are still not hooked up. We processed your truck and came up with nothing. By the way, you can pick it up at impound whenever you want."

"My dad and I will come get it tomorrow," Zeke said.

"Great! I have you on the roster for a week from today. Let me know if it's enough time off, and if it isn't, I can change it if you let me know early enough."

"Thanks. I appreciate the time off. I still get a little wonky when I try to do too much," Zeke admitted.

"He'll rest. Between his mother and I, we'll make sure of it," Tammy said.

"I'm sure you will. I'm heading home for supper. It's pot roast night, my favorite meal."

"Before you go, did you get anything on the thumbprint that was on the gold coin?" Tammy asked.

"What gold coin?" Zeke asked.

"A gold coin Tammy found at the Idle Chat. No, unfortunately, AFIS came up with nothing. We knew it probably wouldn't, as the crime lab guys said they thought it was too smudged to get a clear match."

"You couldn't even rule out Toby Brown or Wilmont Sawyer?"

"We did have Brown's prints on file because of the trouble he got into before, but they didn't match according to the technician."

"What about the prints on the window?"

"There were many partial prints, but nothing concrete enough to use."

"Darn. These people know how to cover their tracks, don't they? At this rate, we'll never find my aunt."

"We'll find Clara. Don't you give up on me and my guys," the sheriff replied.

"I won't. It's just so frustrating."

"Enjoy your pot roast," Zeke said, watching the sheriff climb into his car. "Come on. My mom made her homemade meatloaf swimming in tomato soup. I haven't had it since they moved to Florida."

The four sat down to a nice supper spent telling stories, laughing, and making plans for the upcoming Thanksgiving. Tammy promised if she had her book done and to the publisher, she would join Zeke for the trip. Maggie sent the two younger ones to the living room after supper while she cleaned up the kitchen.

While his parents were in the kitchen, they discussed the recent events of the case. She explained about finding the gold coin in the debris at the shop she had asked the sheriff about earlier. Zeke was extremely upset Brown had assaulted her, and he wasn't there to protect her but did laugh when she described him hobbling away after she stomped on his foot.

They talked for quite a while until Tammy could see Zeke was tiring.

"I'm going home. You need to get some sleep. I'll be writing tomorrow, but I'll give you a call on my lunch break," she promised. "Maybe when you're feeling a little stronger, we can attempt another round of checking out the properties Sawyer owns."

"I'm in, give me another day or so to rest," Zeke whispered. "Just don't tell my mom what we have planned, or she won't let me leave the house."

"It will be our secret."

"When do you think you will hear about your house?"

"I don't think Brown will tie the sale up in any way as he has his eye on some property in Fulton and needs the cash to buy it. I am hoping it will be in the next thirty days. I am waiving the house inspection, or should I say the historical society is, to speed things up even faster. My accountant assured me the money would arrive at my bank within the week."

"Do you really think you can pull this off? You know how the gossip is in this town."

"Only four other people know what is really going on, and now you do, too. Oh, and the sheriff knows. It has to stay a secret for the sale to work. I really love the place. It's gorgeous inside and will take a lot of work to restore it, but it will be so worth it in the end."

"I've never been inside, so I'll take your word for it."

"I can't wait to get the keys so you can see it," Tammy said.

"See what?" Maggie asked, entering the room.

"Tammy's looking at a new car," Zeke said, winking at his girlfriend.

"That's nice. Your dad and I are heading to bed. You should probably do the same, Zeke."

"I was just leaving. Thank you for supper. You'll have to give me the recipe so I can make it for Zeke after you go home."

"I will write it down tomorrow and leave the index card on the fridge. Goodnight."

Zeke put Blinky's leash on and together they walked to Tammy's car. He watched her drive away and then took the dog for a short walk.

Chapter Fourteen

Instead of writing, Tammy spent the morning answering questions for two insurance adjusters who had come to take pictures of the cottage. She told them what she could but admitted they would have to wait to get the bulk of the information they needed from her aunt when she returned.

"If she returns," one of the adjusters mumbled.

"Excuse me?" Tammy demanded.

"I'm just saying. How do we know Clara Beale didn't do this herself for the money and then disappeared? We have to look at claims from every angle."

"Mr.?"

"Ames."

"Mr. Ames, you obviously are not from this area and do not know my aunt or you wouldn't even be thinking those things. My Aunt Clara is an upstanding citizen of Braddock who has lived here all her life. I find it extremely insulting what you are insinuating."

"I'll be in the car," Ames said to his partner.

"I'm so sorry. I know Clara, and it is the furthest thing from my mind she would do something like that. But we received an anonymous phone call to look into this explosion because the person believed Clara did it for the insurance money."

"An anonymous phone call? How convenient," Tammy replied. "My aunt was kidnapped and hasn't been seen since. She was missing before this explosion even happened. You better tell your Mr. Ames he should keep his comments to himself before a lawsuit of libel or slander is filed against him and your company."

"I apologize. I'll file the paperwork, but without your aunt's signature, we can't process it. Here is my card. Please call me when you know anything about Clara."

"I will, thank you, and do me a favor. Don't let Mr. Ames return to this property again, or I will be filing a complaint against your company."

"I understand," he said, walking away.

Tammy shut off the coffee maker and made a list of what she needed at the grocery store. She was still fuming over the rude comments the insurance adjuster made about her aunt. Agitated from the appraiser's meeting, she pulled the list of properties Wilmont Sawyer owned out of her purse and formulated a plan to revisit each place to burn some pent-up energy. The first place she would go was the deserted drive-in where her aunt's sweater had been found.

She pulled on socks over the bottom of her pants legs and laced up her hiking boots. The knee-high socks would help keep the ticks off her, while the boots would protect her feet better than sneakers as she trampled through the woods to get to the more hidden properties. Tammy put new batteries in her flashlight and tucked it in her purse. Her cell phone was at ninety-three percent charged.

Turning down Meadow Lark Lane towards the drive-in, she spotted Hattie and Mabel sitting on the front porch enjoying the morning sunshine. She pulled into their driveway, wanting to tell them they didn't have to worry about Toby Brown anymore, but she couldn't. Not yet, anyway.

"Tammy, we have the best news. Toby Brown is selling the Grady mansion to the historical society, so he won't be bothering us anymore," Hattie announced.

"That's wonderful. How did you find out?"

"Toby Brown told us himself."

He believes the story. That's a good thing.

"Maybe now you will have a little peace around here. No more talk about shotguns, okay?"

"Oh, I was just mad at the time and running my mouth. Besides, Mabel took the gun and hid it somewhere and wouldn't tell me where she put it."

"Good for you, Mabel."

"And where are you off to on this beautiful day?" Hattie asked.

"I'm going hiking. I need to get some exercise after sitting at my computer day after day," she said, not wanting to tell them what she was really doing.

"There's nowhere to hike down this road," Hattie said.

"You caught me. I was really coming over here to check on you, but I guess I won't have to worry about you anymore."

"That's so sweet of you," Mabel said. "Are you going to tell her the news, Hattie, or am I?"

"More news?"

"Mabel is moving here permanently. Isn't that marvelous? She's returning home next week to secure an agent to sell her house."

"That is great. I only have one word of caution for you, Mabel."

"And what is that?"

"Don't let this sister of yours get you into any trouble once you live here. She is quite the gossip, you know," Tammy said, smiling at Hattie. "I speak from experience being someone on the receiving end."

"I apologized to you," Hattie said in a huff.

"Yes, you did," she acknowledged, winking at Mabel.

Hattie saw Tammy wink and took a swing at her with the magazine she was holding.

"You're just giving me a hard time," she said. "Although I do tend to gossip just a little bit."

"I love you anyway," Tammy assured her. "You ladies enjoy the sunshine, and I'll see you shortly. Mabel, good luck selling your house."

The chain across the entrance to the drive-in was sitting on the ground. Tammy drove over it and parked in the field where the poles stood void of the speakers, which once hung on the car windows, enabling people to hear the audio syncing with the picture on the big screen.

The memories came flooding back of her and her parents sitting on the hood of the car, getting eaten by mosquitoes, and munching on popcorn. She missed her mom, and moments like this reminded her just how much she did.

Climbing out of her car, she tucked her phone in the back pocket of her jeans, her keys in her front pocket, and walked toward the first building with her flashlight in hand. The door was partly open, and as she entered, rats and field mice scurried out of sight. It was mostly empty except for a few sections of the long counters where the movie-goers used to push their trays containing the snacks they were going to buy. The cot and various food containers sat in the back corner of the room.

It was obvious from the graffiti on the walls and the empty beer bottles scattered about the local kids were using the place as a hangout. Most of the windows had been smashed, and the light wind outside whistled through the broken glass pieces remaining in the panes.

This is the building where my aunt's sweater was found. I don't see how she could have been held here with the rodent infestation and the teenagers going in and out. Maybe Sawyer was right. Maybe her clothes were placed here to frame him.

The two smaller buildings on the property were locked. Tammy could see through the busted windows the buildings were totally empty. The ticket booth had collapsed, and Tammy was sure no one could have been hidden in the pile of debris sitting there.

On to the next spot.

Her cell phone rang. It was Zeke. She didn't answer it because she didn't want to have to explain where she was or what she was doing. He needed his rest and didn't need to be chasing her down. She let it go to voicemail.

Five of the properties had changed a bit since she and Zeke had been there. The last place she checked out was the cabin on the lake. Cars were parked in the driveway, and people were down on the edge of the lake.

Zeke was right. This must be one of Sawyer Realty's summer rentals. Aunt Clara definitely isn't being held here.

She was depressed she hadn't uncovered anything new, so she headed home to shower and check herself over for any ticks who decided to attach themselves for a free meal. As she was driving home, she happened to look down and see one of the little critters crawling up her leg. She opened her window and threw it out.

Those things give me the creeps. Ticks were one thing we didn't have to worry about in the city.

Before she entered the cabin, she checked herself over to see if there were any more ticks. She didn't want to drag them into the house. Grabbing two towels, she walked around to the back of the cabin.

It's about time I tried the outdoor shower. Aunt Clara loves it and uses it all summer.

Tammy enjoyed herself immensely. It was nice to be able to look up and see the blue sky and listen to the birds as she relaxed under the stream of warm water. An outdoor shower was going to be a must-have addition at her new house.

Now that she was tick-free, she sat down to get in a couple hours of writing. Before she started, she listened to Zeke's voicemail. They were going to The Brown Bear Café for supper and wanted her to join them. She texted him back and said she would meet them there.

The landline rang. Tammy ran to answer it, but when she said hello, no one answered her back. Muffled noises were audible in the background, and then the line went dead. She knew it had to be her aunt trying to reach out to her.

Writing her own crime books, she knew the phone call wasn't long enough to trace, but she did text the sheriff and tell him about it. He texted back, asking if there was a tape to pick up, and she said no, as she had answered the call and not let it go to the answering machine.

Returning to her computer, she had only written a couple of sentences when her cell phone rang. This time, she recognized the number of the person calling.

"Hello."

"Tammy, this is Sylvia. We just had a meeting with Toby Brown and his attorney. He's moving extremely fast because he doesn't want to lose the other property in Fulton. Your attorney was there also, and he will probably be calling you shortly. Mr. Brown signed off on the offer, and because you are offering an all-cash sale, waiving all the inspections, and taking the house as is, they want to close on the sale seven days from now. Is that acceptable to you?"

"Was it acceptable to my attorney?"

"He looked over the contracts and seemed pleased with the terms."

"The money will arrive at my bank shortly. I will be in touch with you after I talk to my attorney," Tammy said. "Thank you for being the frontman."

"It's kind of fun pulling one over on the miserable snake."

"I know what you mean," Tammy agreed.

"Toby Brown doesn't care about anything but money and himself, which I don't understand because his parents are good people. Oh, well. Once you restore the mansion, I'm sure you will love living there. And I can't wait to start the ground penetrating radar in the back yard."

"It will be exciting to see what you find. I've got so many ideas for the inside of the place. I can't wait until I have the keys in my hand, and it's mine."

"I'll let you go. I have another meeting to attend. Thank you again, and I'll keep you appraised of things as they happen."

"I appreciate that. Bye."

Tammy tried hard to get some words down, but she couldn't concentrate. She couldn't shake the feeling she was missing something. Something so simple she just kept skimming over it. Sawyer moved on, as did Brown. Neither one needed to buy Idle Chat anymore, so why hadn't her aunt been released? There had to be more to this.

The thing bothering Tammy the most was who the silent partner was. Why was he hiding from everyone? If people around town saw him, would they know him? At first, she thought it was Brown's mother helping her son behind his father's back, but Tammy learned her social stature and luxurious lifestyle were far too important to her to jeopardize it.

The guy with the long hair had to be the silent partner. Why else wouldn't he want to be seen close-up at the restaurant? She wouldn't recognize him, but maybe Zeke would, and that's why he had to run. He was the key to this mystery and someone Tammy had to concentrate on finding. Tomorrow, she would return to Flashpoint Realty and push for answers.

Locking the door to leave for the restaurant, her phone quaked. The sheriff was messaging her to let her know they had found the shed Zeke had been held in and it wasn't far from Clara's cabin, less than a mile away. It was tied to a property, Flashpoint Realty, held in trust.

Another connection to Toby Brown. How was he going to wiggle his way out of this one?

The Brown Bear was extremely busy. It was a warm summer night during tourist season, and a line of people formed outside the café, waiting for their names to be called and seated. Zeke and his parents were sitting at a patio table enjoying cocktails. Toni Simms, the hostess, spotted a familiar face and asked Tammy if she wanted a cocktail while she waited. She ordered one and went to join her party.

"Have you ever seen the café this busy?" Tammy asked as she sat down.

"You can tell you have been away for a while. It's like this every summer," Zeke answered.

"Peters, party of four," Toni called.

"That would be us. I can't wait to get one of those Reubens in front of me," Will said, standing up. "I think I miss those the most living in Florida."

"Thanks, Dad. I've been replaced by a sandwich," Zeke said.

"Can I talk to Zeke a moment before we join you?" Tammy requested.

"Sure. Do you know what you want to eat, and we will order for you in case the waitress comes to the table before you get there?" Maggie asked.

"A Reuben and extra crispy French fries," they both answered at the same time.

"You'll fit right into this family fine," Will said, laughing.

Tammy blushed at his words.

"Yes, she will," Zeke replied as his parents walked away. "Now tell me what's happening."

"I didn't want to upset your mother by talking about your kidnapping. The sheriff found the shed you were held in, and it was on a property held in a trust by Flashpoint Realty."

"And I was whacked in the parking lot right near their office. Everything points to Toby Brown. I keep wracking my brain trying to think of what I could have seen, but I can't come up with anything."

"You must have seen something; you just aren't putting two and two together yet. Did you exit the mall through the back way and pass by Flashpoint?"

"I did, but the blinds were drawn, and I couldn't see anything. I did hear two people arguing inside."

"Did you recognize the voices?"

"No. They were too muffled."

"Someone must have thought you heard them and could identify them."

"Could be. It makes the most sense so far."

"Wait a minute. That was when Toby Brown was gone all day and night to the seminar. So, who was in the office arguing?"

"The silent partner and someone else," Zeke surmised.

"Now we have two unknowns," Tammy said, frowning.

"Let's go enjoy our supper, and we'll talk more about this later."

Between Zeke, his dad, and Tammy, they used a three-inch-high pile of napkins while they ate their messy Reubens. Will ordered another round of drinks and ordered a hamburger to go for Blinky.

"Really? A burger for the dog?" Zeke asked.

"He's my buddy now, and he told me he wanted a burger," Will said, keeping a straight face.

"He told you? My husband is such a sucker when it comes to animals," Maggie said.

"I know," he replied. "And you wouldn't change me even if you could."

"I'm going to walk Tammy to her car. I'll be right back," Zeke said.

"Doc says I'm clear to drive starting tomorrow. Maybe we can revisit the properties Sawyer owns and see if we can find any additional ones Brown owns."

"Beat you to it. I went to the places we checked already, and there were no changes."

"You went by yourself?"

"I was fine. The only scary thing I ran into was all the ticks that managed to find their way up my legs," she replied.

166

"Please promise me you won't go out by yourself again. These people aren't messing around. Look what they did to me, and I'm a lot bigger in stature than you are."

"I won't. There are too many unknowns to deal with now."

"Go home and lock the door behind you. I'll call you tomorrow."

It was only a quarter to eight when Tammy arrived home. Too early to go to bed, she sat on the porch with a wine cooler to watch what was left of the sunset. Now that the insurance adjusters had been to the cottage to take pictures, she would get up in the morning and take a bunch of her own on her phone for her aunt.

Then, she would call for a commercial dumpster to be delivered by a company she had found online and seemed reputable so she could start the clean-up process. After the explosion and the fire that followed it, there wasn't much left that would end up in the dumpster.

The mosquitoes were coming out in droves. Tammy retreated into the cabin to save herself. She sat down to work on a simple outline for a second book she was considering writing. This was the way her mind worked. It was always ready to start on a new book even though she was in the middle of writing a different one. When her eyes started stinging from staring at the computer screen, she called it quits and went to bed.

As the sun came up, she filled her travel mug with coffee and grabbed her phone. Walking across the backyard, she noticed she had neglected the bird feeders, and three of the four were empty. Turning around, she walked back to the far side of the porch and opened the metal trash barrel holding the birdseed. By the time she was done filling the last one, the birds had already found their new food in the first one.

Walking around the burnt-out structure, taking pictures from different angles, she noticed something hanging from a tree at the back perimeter of the yard. After she took a picture of its exact location, she found a long branch to knock it down out of the tree. It was a wig, a black, long-haired wig. It looked exactly like the hair the silent partner had.

I bet this blew off in the force of the explosion. He must have been the one who set the bomb and the one Zeke chased through the woods.

167

Not wanting to touch it, she ran back to the cabin to get some plastic gloves and a bag to put it in. Hurrying back to the spot where she left it sitting on the ground, she couldn't find it anywhere. She perused the whole area, and it was gone. She felt a chill go right up her spine.

Someone was watching me and took off with the wig.

Tammy called the sheriff to tell him what happened. She informed him she was sure it was Toby Brown's silent partner who was watching her and ran off with the evidence when she went back to the cabin. Now they knew it wasn't his real hair but a disguise to hide his identity even more. It was time to make another trip to Flashpoint Realty.

Driving to the mall, Tammy ran a scenario through her head that she would use once she arrived at her destination. Parking at the front of the mall so she wouldn't be seen entering the building and so she could approach the office without being seen out the bay window overlooking the back parking lot, she hid in the store across the way from the door of the realty office. The blinds were open, but it was in total darkness inside. She watched for a few more minutes, and after seeing no movement, she approached the realty office door. The door was locked.

Shielding her eyes from the fluorescent lights above her, she peered into the office through the glass door. A figure was crouching behind the receptionist's desk in the dark. Whoever was there was trying very hard to be still and not to be seen.

Let's see if I can startle them into moving.

"I know you're in there," she yelled, banging on the door. "I can see you behind the desk!"

The figure dropped to all fours and crawled toward the offices in the back. Tammy banged a few more times and gave up before she drew a crowd or mall security. The person in the office could stay in there all day. Or, while she was watching one entrance, they could sneak out the other. She returned to the business across the way and kept an eye on the office for another twenty minutes before giving up. Purchasing a pair of flip-flops to use in the outdoor shower, she exited the store and returned to her car.

While she was in town, Tammy stopped at the hardware store to check on the keys she had ordered and to buy a couple of gallons of concrete sealer for the Idle Chat floor. Many colors were available, but she chose a royal blue, which was dark enough to cover the blood stains yet nice to look at. The peacock keys were still unavailable.

Her next order of business was to visit Sawyer Realty. Parked in the lot across the street, she pulled out her trusty binoculars and checked to see who was in the office before she entered. Sally was busy shuffling papers, and Wilmont was going back and forth from his office to her desk.

Let's go in and get this over with.

Tammy opened the door, and when Wilmont saw her, he frowned.

"It's nice to see you again, too, Mr. Sawyer," she said.

"What do you want, Miss Wright? We are extremely busy today and don't have time for your stories."

"My stories? My how your attitude has changed over the last week," she noted.

"What do you want?"

"I want the address of the new property you purchased for your condo development. My aunt is still missing, and we are checking every avenue looking for her."

"I have told you repeatedly I had nothing to do with Clara's disappearance, but yet you persist," he grumbled. "Sally, write down the address of the new property and give it to her."

"Mr. Sawyer, do you know Toby Brown has also moved on and is selling the Grady mansion to the historical society? He and his silent partner are buying property in Fulton."

"Being a top agent means I have to know everything going on in my community. I know every step Brown is making, and don't you think I don't. I have enough on my plate with the new mini-mall construction at the drive-in and my condo development to worry about a second-rate realtor like Brown and his dealings."

"So, you are telling me if his deals go through and he makes a good amount of money off the sales of the houses, you won't try to recoup any of the money you lost?" Tammy asked.

"We tried once," Sally answered. "There is nothing we can do to my brother to get the money back. The law was on his side. Legally, we can't touch him. I don't want to see him become successful after all the rotten things he has done. Truthfully, I hope he falls flat on his face and loses everything."

"He'll get his. I just hope I'm around to see it happen," Wilmont mumbled. "Now, is there anything else?"

"No, that's it," she said, taking the slip of paper from Sally.

"Good, now leave. We have a lot of work to do," he said, opening the door.

"Have a wonderful day, Mr. Sawyer," she said sarcastically.

He slammed the door in her face.

He knows everything going on in town. What a joke. Mr. Big Shot doesn't know I'm buying the Grady mansion and not the historical society.

Her cell rang.

"Hello, Sheriff," she answered.

"I wanted to let you know we heard back from the crime lab in regard to the explosive device used to blow up your cottage."

"And?"

"The agent told me that because of the complexity of the wiring and the type of timer used, the bomb was built by a demolition expert. It wasn't something you could get instructions for on the internet."

"Is there anyone in town you know of who has this kind of expertise?"

"No one I know of locally. There's four guys on the Fulton Bomb Squad who have the knowledge, but I've known each one of them for many years and can't see any of them involved in something like this."

"This silent partner gets more intense with each bit of information we discover about him."

"I know I've said it before, but I will say it again. Be careful."

"I will. I have an appointment with my attorney at noon. I'll be at the Braddock Diner if you need me."

"Okay. Bye."

Tammy's meeting with her attorney went well. They ate their lunch and discussed everything she had to know about the sale and the trust he set up for her, which required her signature on several legal documents so it could be filed.

"The trust is in the name of TW Trust, not that Brown cared at all. His main interest was for the cashier's check to be made out correctly to Flashpoint Realty."

"Sounds like him. I'm still trying to figure out if he's going to scam his new partner and take off with the money like he did to his sister and Wilmont Sawyer."

"We're meeting at nine o'clock on Friday morning at the historical society office. He has no idea the mansion will be sold directly to you. Make sure when you go to the bank to get the check, you don't let them list your name in the memo. Have them put Grady mansion sale to TW Trust instead."

"Okay. So, as soon as you hand over the check, the place is mine?"

"I have filed the appropriate paperwork with The Registry of Deeds to change the name. As I have power of attorney for you, I will act as the representative for the trust and sign what is needed for the sale to transpire."

"I don't have to be there at all?"

"Correct."

"You have no idea how excited I am to own this house."

"Am I to assume you will not be returning to New York?"

"I am not. I can write here just as well as there. And I have a new relationship here. Someone I was interested in years ago, but things didn't work out then," Tammy said, smiling.

"I am happy for you."

"Here's your bill. Have a great day," the waitress said.

"Thank you, and to you also. Call me when you get the check from the bank, and I'll come pick it up," her attorney said, standing up. "By this time next week, you will be the proud owner of Grady mansion."

"I'd like to change the name back to Blackstone Manor after the original builder and owner, Jedidiah Blackstone."

"There's no reason you can't. Names are assigned to represent who owns the property at that specific time. You can call your residence by any name you would like. Lunch is on me today," he said, grabbing the bill.

"Thank you," Tammy replied.

"Let's see if you're still thanking me when you get my bill for services," he said, chuckling.

"That bad, huh?"

"Just wait and see," he said, walking away.

Every cent spent will be well worth it.

Returning home, Tammy spent the next several hours concentrating on her writing. Proud of what she had accomplished, she texted Zeke to see what he was doing. Returning an answer almost immediately, he begged to be rescued. When she asked what he meant, he explained that his mother wanted to check out the new mall and that he was following her from store to store and carrying her bags. Zeke hated shopping. He continued texting her telling her they were going out to dinner with some old family friends, and he would call her in the morning.

She told him she would be painting the Idle Chat floor in the morning and would love his company if he felt up to it. He promised to meet her there at nine o'clock. She typed goodbye.

Wanting to find out more about the gold coins she found at the mansion, she retrieved them from the safe and searched online for more information. The California Gold Coins, which were actually considered ingots, as the sheriff had already told her, were produced from 1849 to 1856. The ones Tammy had found in the fireplace were all dated 1852.

The majority of the coins remained and were used west of the Mississippi River, especially in the area now known as California, but some did manage to find their way to the East Coast as people returned from the Gold Rush.

The value of the coins themselves was hard to pin down by looking at pictures on the computer. It all depended on the condition of the coin. These looked to be uncirculated and must have been hidden in the house when they were first obtained. She would have to take them to an expert for their true value.

These would look cool framed and mounted above the fireplace where they were found.

Wrapping each one individually in a soft cloth, she returned them to their hiding place.

Since she arrived in Braddock, she had gotten out of the habit of cooking a big meal for herself. Vegetables had been only part of her diet if she ate out at a restaurant. Rummaging through the refrigerator, she pulled out ingredients to make herself a vegetable plate. A fresh ear of corn steamed in the microwave, mashed summer squash with butter, salt, and pepper, and a meaty tomato she would slice up and lather with mayo was the healthiest meal she had eaten in a while.

Setting her fork down and staring at the empty chair on the other side of the kitchen table, Tammy's heart ached. Her aunt was no spring chicken, feisty, yes, but not young. She had been gone a long time. Too long. Were they feeding her? How was her health holding up? She was skinny to begin with and couldn't afford to lose too much more weight.

What good is writing mysteries if it doesn't even help me to figure out where my aunt is or who has her?

Tammy resumed eating her supper, forcing each bite down as she went. Halfway through, she gave up. Leaving the plate on the table, she crawled onto her aunt's bed, hugging her pillow and pulling a quilt over herself. She eventually fell asleep while crying.

Chapter Fifteen

Tammy woke up to swollen eyes and blotchy skin. Looking at herself in the mirror, she knew she needed to put on some make-up to hide her breakdown from the night before, but all her cosmetics had been lost in the fire, and she hadn't replaced them yet. She was due to meet Zeke in twenty minutes and didn't have time to run into town to get new stuff.

He was already in the parking lot when Tammy arrived. She knew she looked awful, but if they were going to be dating, Zeke would have to accept the good with the bad, and today was the bad. She saw his smile turn into a frown when he got his first glimpse of her face. She wanted to run back to the car and drive away as fast as she could.

"Are you okay?" he asked, reaching for her hand.

"It was a tough night," she whispered.

"Why didn't you call me? I would have come over."

"And watch me cry like a blubbering idiot? I don't think so."

"You're not a blubbering idiot. You're a strong woman who has a lot on her mind, and it all caught up to you at once, that's all. Everyone has to release their emotions somehow."

"And how do you release yours?"

"I have a punching bag hanging in the garage I tend to beat the stuffing out of when I need to blow off steam."

"I'm sorry I look like this. My make-up was destroyed in the fire and if I still had it, I wouldn't look this bad."

"You don't look bad, okay, maybe a little bad. Let's not talk about it anymore and get to work instead. Did you bring the sealer?"

"It's in my car."

"I'll get it while you unlock the door," he offered.

The first coat of sealer had been applied to the loading dock and kiln room floors. The blue brightened up the place, but the floor would need a second coat to cover up the faint traces of the remaining blood stains. They would return the following morning and give it a second and final coat.

"Want to go look at my new residence? Well, it will be as of Friday morning."

"Sure, I haven't been down to the Grady mansion for a while."

"It's not going to be known as the Grady mansion once I own it. I'm going back to the name of Blackstone Manor."

"Jedidiah will be happy. He does haunt the place you know, or didn't they tell you that before you bought it?"

"That's just a story you guys made up to scare us girls at Halloween."

"Maybe, maybe not."

They joined hands and started walking toward the house. Hattie and Mabel were sitting on their front porch.

"Hello, neighbor!" Hattie yelled.

"She called me neighbor," Tammy whispered to Zeke. "How does she know I bought the house?"

"Maybe she's referring to the ceramic shop," he suggested.

"Let's find out," she said, pulling Zeke up the walk toward the porch where the women were sitting.

"Good morning," Zeke said.

"It does my heart good to see you smiling and living your life again, Zeke Peters. The whole town was worried about you after your break-up with Emily. And now, she's back in town again. You stay clear of her, you hear me. You have got a good girl here. Don't mess it up," Hattie lectured.

"Yes, ma'am."

"Hattie, stop telling people what to do," Mabel said.

Maybe someday you'll live next door, too?" Hattie asked.

"Excuse me?"

"If you and Tammy get married, will you move in with her at the mansion?"

"Hattie! Honestly," Mabel said, rolling her eyes at her sister.

"How do you know I'm moving in there?"

"The whole town knows, dear. Toby Brown overheard Sylvia talking to you on the phone at the historical society. It was a nice try putting the property into a trust so Brown wouldn't know it was you purchasing the place."

"I don't believe this. We were so careful to keep this a secret," Tammy said.

"Don't worry about it. Brown doesn't care it was you, he just wanted the money from the sale. He bragged about some big deal he was going to make millions from once he got your check."

"And he told you all this?"

"Yes, he did. Brown was over at the mansion yesterday taking out a few last-minute things, and he couldn't help himself not to come over here to brag."

"I hope he didn't take the tin ceilings or the chandelier in the library."

"We kept an eye on him," Mabel said. "It was all small items except for the one extra-large garment bag he had slung over his shoulder and then tossed it in the backseat of his car."

Tammy's stomach sank. Could it have been her aunt in the bag? Was Clara in the house the whole time she was there for the estate sale? If so, where was she hidden, and why didn't she cry out for help?

Zeke knew exactly what she was thinking because he was thinking the same thing. Because Brown knew Tammy was buying the house, they could go and confront him on the issue of what was in the white bag.

"Let's go," Zeke said, taking Tammy's hand. "There's something we have to do."

Leaving her car at the ceramic shop, they drove to Flashpoint Realty. Brown's car was in the parking lot behind the mall. Tammy peered into the car. The white bag was still lying across the seat, and she tried to open the door.

"Hey, what are you doing to my car?" Brown yelled, running toward them. "You!"

"What's in the white bag, Toby?" Zeke asked.

"That's none of your business."

"It is if it's Clara Beale."

"Are you crazy?"

"You were seen removing this bag from the mansion," Zeke stated. "Did you have to move her because of the sale of the house?"

"Are you on the clock? If not, have someone who is and make sure they have a search warrant," he demanded.

"Zeke, the bag hasn't moved. If it is my aunt, there may be something really wrong with her," Tammy said, staring through the window.

"I have told you repeatedly I had nothing to do with Clara's disappearance. And just to avoid further embarrassment of the police showing up here, I'll show you what's in the bag. Move!"

Tammy stepped aside, and Brown unlocked the car. He opened the door and pulled out the bag. The zipper down, Tammy could see brown fur inside.

"These are fur coats I found in the closet underneath the stairs. I figured you didn't own the house yet, so I was free to take them and sell them. Nice try attempting to buy the house under a trust name. It might have worked if Sylvia didn't have such a big mouth and was a little more careful about who was around listening to her when she talked on the phone."

"I didn't want the house torn down. It's a part of Braddock's history," Tammy said.

"I could give two flaps about history. I still would have sold the house even if I knew it was you as long as you met my selling price. Have fun living in that dump when you could have bought a brand-new build from me."

"Live in a cookie-cutter house? No thanks."

"Those cookie-cutter houses, as you call them, are going to make me a millionaire once I get the check from you and buy property in Fulton. Just make sure you make the check payable to Flashpoint Realty."

"Everything I'm hearing is I. Doesn't your silent partner have a say in anything?" Tammy asked.

"He's my lackey. I tell him what to do, and he does it. That idiot doesn't have the first clue about real estate, but he had the money I needed for start-up costs."

"Why is he being so secretive?"

"Beats me. If he wants to hand over money, he can be as secretive as he wants to be. Now, are you satisfied? Can I return to work?"

"I guess," Tammy said.

"I may have done some low things in my life, but I would never stoop to kidnapping. Just make sure my check is at the historical society on Friday morning," Brown said, walking away.

"I was so sure Aunt Clara was in the bag," Tammy said, sighing.

"We'll find her," Zeke said. "I'll take you back to your car. I promised my parents I'd spend tonight and tomorrow with them as they are leaving in two days. Are you going to be okay?"

"Yeah, I'll be fine. I'll go to the shop tomorrow and put the final coat of sealer down and then get some writing done. I have a dumpster coming next week to start cleaning the cottage area, which will take up a lot of my writing time."

"I'll help on my days off. Do you want to grab a late lunch before I go home?' Zeke asked as they climbed into his truck.

"No, thanks. I'm not really hungry right now."

They drove in silence back to Idle Chat.

"Give me a call tomorrow," Tammy said, hopping down out of the truck.

He drove away, and she felt bad inside. She wasn't in the mood to be sociable even though a few days ago, she could have lost him. Writing wasn't on the top of her list either, but she would make herself sit and meet the daily word count she had set for herself.

She made a BLT with extra bacon for an early supper, and she ate every bit. Pouring herself a glass of wine, she sat at her computer and began to write. Once she freed her mind of stress and worry, the words flowed. Two chapters later, she went to bed.

Stopping at the Brown Bear Café on the way to the ceramic shop, Tammy grabbed a ham and cheese omelet, home fries, wheat toast, and an orange juice. Her coffee was half gone before she arrived at Idle Chat. She took her breakfast and ate at one of the tables in the main classroom. It was quiet and provided her with time to think.

Tammy realized she herself had been a bully to her aunt. Trying to convince her to keep the shop when she didn't want to was just as bad as Sawyer trying to make her sell it. If—no—when her aunt returned, Tammy would back her in whatever she wanted to do in regard to her shop. If she wanted to retire and sell the place to Zee Campbell, then so be it. The area could use a nice hair salon.

The second coat of sealer went on much faster as the floor already had a good base coat. An hour later, she was done, and there were no more telltale signs of Goodwin Scott's murder.

Locking up, she left to go to the bank to pick up the cashier's check. She really wanted to attend the meeting in the morning, seeing as Brown already knew it was her buying the house, but decided against going. Her attorney could deal with it as he had been doing all along.

With the check hidden deep in her purse, she exited the bank. Stopping a few steps outside the door, she looked around. She had an overwhelming feeling she was being watched. Not seeing anyone she knew or anyone who was watching her, she continued to her car.

Maybe you're just being paranoid because of the size of the check.

Starting the car so the doors would lock, she felt safer and relaxed a little more. She texted her attorney, and he agreed to be at her aunt's house when she got there to pick up the check.

That makes me feel better. I don't want the check in my possession any longer than it has to be.

Tomorrow, she would receive her keys to the mansion. Flashpoint Realty had already turned off the electricity and water. Tammy needed to make the necessary calls to get everything hooked up again as soon as possible. There was so much to do, and she couldn't wait to get started.

Zeke was busy with his parents all day, which meant she could spend the entire day writing. When her attorney arrived, she handed him two checks: one for the purchase amount from the bank and a personal check covering the closing costs and fees.

Warning him to be careful as she felt she was being watched as she left the bank, he said he would be on his guard. She also told him Brown knew she was buying the house, so he didn't have to keep up the pretense at the morning meeting. He left with the promise to call her when the meeting concluded.

Zeke called around supper time to check in on her. He laughed as he told her he had been duped into taking his mother to the Portland Flower Show. His father had severe allergies and couldn't take his wife. It was one event she enjoyed attending every year when she lived here. He returned with the back of his truck full of different colored azalea bushes.

Tammy couldn't sleep that night. The excitement of owning the mansion kept her tossing and turning, staring at the ceiling and finally caused her to make a cup of tea at two a.m. Her mind wouldn't shut down long enough to allow her to doze off. New ideas kept presenting themselves for the renovations that needed to be done. Instead of returning to bed, she sat in the recliner with a notebook, drinking her tea and writing down the ideas so she wouldn't forget them.

Tired from sitting up most of the night, but excited for the day ahead of her, she made a pot of coffee and filled the biggest mug she could find. Sitting on the front porch, she waited anxiously for her attorney to call.

Aunt Clara, I wish you were here for my big day of becoming a first-time homeowner. And what a choice I made for my first place. It's magnificent. I miss you so much.

At nine-thirty, the phone rang. She practically leapt out of the rocking chair to get to her cell phone on the picnic table.

"Hello!"

"Congratulations! The mansion is yours!"

"I can't believe it," Tammy squealed.

"Believe it. Do you want to meet me there so I can officially hand you the keys?'

"I'll be there in twenty minutes," she said, hanging up the phone.

Tammy pulled into the circular driveway and inhaled deeply. Staring at the mansion, she couldn't believe it was hers. All hers. Never in her wildest dreams did she see herself owning a place like this. She said a small prayer of thanks to her publisher for her advances and to the readers who bought her books and made this possible with the royalties she had been paid.

Her knees were shaking as she exited her car. She smiled broadly as she approached her attorney, who was dangling a set of keys before her.

"Congratulations! Here you go!"

Her hands were shaking as she reached for the keys and took hold of them.

"I wish my Aunt Clara was here with me," she said. "Would you like to go in and see my new house? My house. I love the sound of that."

"I'll have to take a rain check. I have some papers to file and a few other errands to run. You enjoy your house. You've earned it. By the way, Brown couldn't get out of the office fast enough once he had the check in his hand. It was almost comical watching him fidget in his chair."

"I can imagine," Tammy smiled. "Thank you again for all you have done."

"Any time, Miss Wright, any time," he replied, walking to his car. "I'll talk to you soon."

Standing on the front porch, her anticipation growing with each passing second, she slid the key in the lock and turned it. It's not like she hadn't been in the house before, but this time, she was entering as the owner. A horn beeped behind her, and Zeke's truck pulled into the driveway.

At least I have one person to share my big day with.

"Darn woman, this house is huge," he said.

"It's a mansion, not a house," she replied, sticking her nose in the air, pretending to be snotty.

"Well, excuse me. This mansion is huge," he said, laughing.

She ran to him and gave him a big hug.

You need to buy a house more often if this is how I get greeted," he said, smiling.

"Isn't it beautiful? Or it will be when it's fully restored."

"I haven't been here since we were kids."

"You make us sound so old. It was only ten, twelve years ago."

"I guess it wasn't so long ago. Where do you want me to put them?"

"Put what?" Tammy asked, confused at the question.

"All the azalea bushes in the back of my truck," he answered.

181

"You got those for me?"

"I did. They're a housewarming gift. I figured they'd look good lining the driveway. That is, if you like azaleas."

"I love them. Especially the purple ones."

"We'll need to do some yard work before we plant them. It shouldn't take any more than a few days to whip this outside space into shape."

"We?"

"You can't do everything yourself, even if you think you can."

"I know. I've been on my own since graduation. City living is so different than here in Braddock. There are millions of people around you, but you are still by yourself. Give me time, and I'll return to my old Braddock ways."

"Have you been inside yet?"

"I was just opening the door when you pulled in and honked. Do you want to see it?"

"Yes, ma'am."

They stepped inside and stood in the foyer. The leftovers from the estate sale were scattered about the place, along with lots of trash. Tammy hadn't seen any signs of rodents when she walked around the day of the sale but would call an exterminator to check the place from top to bottom.

"Come on, I want to check to see if Brown actually left the place as is and left the items I wanted for the restoration."

The library hadn't been disturbed since she left the day of the sale. The chandelier still hung in the center of the room, surrounded by the detailed tin ceiling. The built-in bookcases didn't need to be refinished. They just needed a good cleaning before her collection of books could be displayed.

"You are now standing in the center of my new writing office," she said proudly. "What do you think?"

"Unbelievable."

"My first step is to get someone in here to test for lead paint. I'm sure almost all the paint used in the house is lead-based because of its age. That process alone may take weeks if it all has to be stripped and the surfaces treated."

"Are you going to stay at Clara's until you can move in?"

"I don't think so. When she comes home, you notice I did say when, she is used to living by herself and is set in her ways. With no cottage left, I may rent a room at the bed and breakfast in town until I can move in here."

"You might want to hold off renting a room. Depending on Clara's condition, when she is found, she might need someone around until she returns to her old self."

"I wouldn't dream of leaving her alone until I know she will be fine and able to function on her own again. And I made the decision whatever she chooses to do in regard to the ceramic shop, I will back her one hundred percent," Tammy replied.

"After all that has happened to her recently, it might be good for her to sell the place and retire. She deserves it."

"I want to show you something upstairs."

Tammy showed Zeke the hole where she found the coins hidden in the fireplace. They walked from room to room, discussing what needed to be done for the mansion to be livable. He was glad that she was keeping the tin ceilings, and for the most part, they were still intact.

She asked his advice on whether or not he thought the rooms were big enough to install small bathrooms in each one, as she wanted to hold author retreats at the place when it was finished. He felt there was plenty of room, but it would be expensive to do as there was no existing plumbing except for the pipes connected to the heating system.

They were poking around in the kitchen area when Zeke's cell phone rang. "Hello."

He didn't say anything. He just listened to what was being said on the other end.

"We'll be right there!"

"Who was that?" Tammy asked.

"It was Sheriff Becker. He's been trying to reach you, but you didn't pick up."

"My cell is in the car. I was so excited about getting the keys to my own place I left it on the front seat."

"They have arrested Toby Brown. An anonymous tip was called into the police station that Clara was being held at the bowling alley. Brown was in his office when they stormed the place. They found your aunt in a small room at the back of the cellar. She's been drugged, but they don't know with what or how much. An ambulance is taking her to the hospital as we speak."

"I'll drive. Let's go!" she said.

Tammy broke every speed limit to get to the hospital. The couple ran into the emergency room entrance, where Sheriff Becker was standing at the check-in desk waiting for them to arrive.

"Where's my aunt? I need to see her," Tammy said. "Is she going to be okay?"

"Slow down. The doctors are still checking her over. Her vital signs are good, but she is out cold from whatever they sedated her with."

"When can I see her?"

"Soon. Doc says he'll come out and get us when she starts to come to."

"I can't believe she was at the bowling alley this whole time," Tammy said.

"That's the funny thing, she wasn't. We searched there earlier, and Clara wasn't there."

"Brown had her stashed somewhere else and moved her there later after you had searched the place?" Zeke asked.

"Looks like it," the sheriff replied. "The weird thing is, he claims he had no knowledge of her being down in the cellar."

"Of course, it's what he's going to say. He got caught," Tammy said.

"No, his reactions were consistent with a person in total shock when he saw Clara being brought upstairs on the gurney. He swore up and down he didn't know how she got there."

"Zeke said you received an anonymous tip?" Tammy asked.

"A male called the tip in. He said he was at the store across the street buying beer and saw Brown carrying a body in through the back door of the bowling alley."

"Brown was set up," Tammy stated.

"Why do you say that?" Zeke asked.

"Remember when I staked out the bowling alley? You can't see the back door from the liquor store across the street. It can only be seen from the adjacent parking lot of the business next door, which is where I sat taking my pictures."

"I still have to question him. For now, I am holding him on kidnapping and abuse of an elder. He'll spend the weekend in jail and go in front of the judge on Monday if charged."

"Don't let my aunt hear you call her an elder. She'll set you straight in no uncertain terms," Tammy warned.

"That she would," the sheriff agreed.

"You can see Clara now. She's still groggy, but she wants to talk to you," Doc said, walking up to the group. "Don't stay more than a few minutes. She's in cubicle five."

"We'll be in the waiting room," Zeke said.

Tammy followed the doctor through the doors. He pointed in the direction of where she needed to go. The curtain was closed. Tammy peeked in and let out a sigh of relief at seeing her aunt lying there.

She was pale and had definitely lost some weight. Her hair was flat and matted, not its usual curly style. Tammy didn't care what she looked like, and she was grateful that her aunt had been found and returned to her safe and sound. Clara opened her eyes and waved her niece forward.

"Aunt Clara," Tammy said, taking her aunt's frail hand.

"No tears," she told her niece, wiping away a tear as it slid down Tammy's cheek.

"I was so worried about you."

"I was worried about me," she said, joking around. "You didn't seriously think I would let anyone get the better of me, did you?"

"I told Zeke you were feisty. Do you know who it was who held you captive or where you were kept?"

"I don't have a clue to either. The last thing I remember is someone coming up behind me in the cabin and putting a funny-smelling cloth over my face. I woke up hours later, locked in a dark room with no windows. I felt my way around the room and found a flashlight sitting on the floor. There was a toilet in the corner of the room, but it didn't even flush."

"That's disgusting."

"It was, but at least I received meals three times a day, and the food wasn't bad. It wasn't home-cooked; everything came from a restaurant in to-go containers."

"At least they fed you. Did you ever hear anyone talking?" Any voices?"

"No, none. The last meal I ate made me feel strange. Then, I woke up here. Doc says they found me in the bowling alley cellar. Is that true?"

"It is."

"I don't think I was there the whole time. I'm sure I would have heard the reset machines slamming on the floor above me. The last meal must have had something in it knocking me out, and I was moved right before I was found."

"At least your home now; that's all that counts."

"Is it true? Did they blow up my cottage?"

"How do you know that?" Tammy asked.

"They left pictures of it in my room while I was sleeping. I was so afraid you were in it when it happened. I banged on the door and begged for them to tell me if you were okay, but they never answered me."

"Zeke and I thought they were going to use it to make you sell Idle Chat."

"That's the weird part. Never once was I approached to sell the shop. They never even spoke to me."

"You keep saying they. Do you know it was more than one person?"

"No, I don't," she said, sighing.

"You get some rest now. I'll pass on everything you said to the sheriff. Doc says he's going to keep you overnight to keep an eye on you, but you can go home tomorrow."

"Really? I want to go home and take a nice shower and sleep in my own bed."

"We have to make sure you have no adverse effects from the drugs they used. Eat a good supper, get some sleep, and I'll be back in the morning to bring you home. Deal?"

"I am tired. Deal," she said.

"I'll see you then. Aunt Clara, I'm so happy you're home. I love you."

"I love you, too."

Tammy joined the two men in the waiting room. She repeated everything her aunt had said to the sheriff as she promised. Knowing Clara was safe and staying for the night, he left to go question Toby Brown.

"I hate to say this, but I need you to take me back to my truck so I can get home. My parents are leaving in the morning, and I promised we'd go out to dinner together."

"That's fine. I told my aunt I wouldn't be back until the morning. I could tell she was tired and needed to rest. I'm going to spruce up the cabin and put clean linen on her bed. I want everything to be perfect when she comes home."

"Sounds like a plan," he said, opening the car door for her.

Tammy sat at the mansion after Zeke left. She couldn't wait to tell her aunt she was staying put in Braddock, and she bought herself a house. It would be a happy topic of discussion over dinner tomorrow night.

The cabin was cleaned and ready for Clara's return when Tammy finally went to bed. She would do a quick shopping trip in the morning, so her aunt had food in the house. She wouldn't have to exert herself and could relax for the first few days she was home without driving anywhere.

Her aunt was resting comfortably in her recliner by eleven o'clock the next day. Tammy made her a nice lunch, and Clara went to lie down in her room after she ate. Zeke was taking his parents to the airport, so Tammy had a little time to kill before she had to make the two women supper.

I think I'll pay Mr. Sawyer a visit and see if he knows it was me who bought the mansion and if he knows my aunt is home. We still don't know who held her captive, and his reaction to the news of her safety should tell a story.

Sawyer Realty was empty when Tammy entered. She could hear Wilmont talking on the phone in his office and decided to quietly wait for him to come out. Walking to the picture wall, she scrutinized each picture and then moved on to the next.

Hearing Sawyer end his phone call, she hurried to the reception desk as if she had been waiting for him to come out.

"Tammy! Is it true? Is Clara home?"

"Yes, it's true. They found her at the bowling alley yesterday."

"Toby Brown had her. What a scumbag. You all thought it was me, but I knew all along it was him."

"He says he didn't do it."

"Yeah, right," he said, hanging a set of keys above Sally's desk.

It was then Tammy saw it. The missing peacock key was hanging amongst some keys already on the board.

"That is a lot of keys," she said, pointing to the ring holding Clara's key. "You'd have trouble keeping your pants up walking around with those in your pocket."

"Those are Sally's keys. She usually carries them in her purse, but she's leaving for vacation on Monday, and I may need duplicate keys, so she's leaving them here," he said, showing no signs of panic. The key was there to be seen.

"Those are Sally's?"

"That's what I said. Why?"

"No, reason. You don't see a woman carry around a large set of keys very often. Her purse must have weighed a ton."

"She was used to it. She very rarely took them out of her purse."

Either she forgot about the key being on there, or she doesn't care if it is seen because she has no intention of returning here after vacation.

"I came here to admit to you it was me who bought the Grady mansion not the historical society. I'm going to restore the place and stay in Braddock."

"I know. Sally told me it was you, and you paid triple the value of the taxes due when the mansion was auctioned off."

Strike two, Sally. No one but the people at the closing and the silent partner could have known what I paid for it.

"Where is Sally going on vacation?"

"She's always talked about going to the south of France and visiting wine country there. I assume it's where she's going, although she never really mentioned a particular destination."

"Thank you, Mr. Sawyer, you have been very helpful. Have a nice day."

Tammy rushed outside to call the sheriff.

"I know who kidnapped my aunt and why they did it. Can you meet me at my aunt's cabin in half an hour?" she asked the sheriff.

Chapter Sixteen

Tammy was waiting on the front porch for the sheriff when he arrived. She hadn't gone inside because she didn't want to wake up her aunt.

"What's this about, you know who kidnapped Clara?" he asked, sitting down in the rocker next to her.

"I need you to verify something for me first. You have to call Camp Campbell in Virginia and find out if Wilmont's son Mark is still stationed there. He supposedly has been overseas and is returning home on leave after Christmas."

"Did Wilmont tell you where his son was, and what has he got to do with this?"

"No. I saw the name of the base where he is stationed on his picture on the wall at the realty office. His clean-shaven face looked very familiar to me. He was wearing the pin of an Army Explosive Ordinance Officer. My dad disabled bombs in the Reserves, and I recognized the symbols on the pin above his uniform pocket."

"Ah, the explosion at the cottage. I don't get it, though. If he's overseas, how can he be mixed up in this?"

"I don't think he is overseas anymore; that's why I need you to call the base. I think he's home and has been working with Sally Pratt to get even with Toby for the money she lost in the vineyard fiasco. He's been disguising himself with a wig and bushy facial hair so no one would recognize him and tell his parents he was here."

"Why do you think Sally is in on this?"

190

"I was just at Sawyer Realty and saw my aunt's missing peacock key hanging on a ring above Sally's desk. Wilmont confirmed they were hers, and she usually kept them stashed in her purse, except now she's going on vacation and left the keys behind. He showed no reaction whatsoever when I chatted about the key ring. Those keys were specially made for my aunt and there are no others like them in this area, so it has to be Goodwin's key."

"Before we go any further, I want to call the base and see what they have to say."

"Fine, but we have to act fast."

"Why?'

"Because I think they set up Brown to get him out of the way so the silent partner, who I believe to be Mark Sawyer, can empty the joint account of Flashpoint Realty of the money from the Grady sale on Monday morning when the bank opens, and the check has cleared. I also know Brown has secured additional investor money for his project from my search online which is probably in the account also. They will be long gone before Toby Brown is released from jail."

"May I use Clara's landline to make the call instead of wasting time going all the way back to my office?'

"You sure can," Clara answered from behind the screen door. "They left me in a dark room for days with a toilet that didn't even flush just for money? Sally's mother and I were good friends right up until the church fiasco, when she shut herself away from anyone she was close to at the time. It frosts my cake that her daughter would do this to me. Harry, you make sure you get them."

"We will. Now, let me make that call."

Tammy and Clara sat outside while the sheriff placed the call to Virginia. He returned twenty minutes later.

"I couldn't get too much info, but they did verify Mark Sawyer had been dishonorably discharged three months ago and returned to the States. I asked what for, but they wouldn't give me any details except for the fact he was a key witness for JAG and received immunity for his testimony. He didn't go to federal prison like the other soldiers who were involved."

"Why would he come home and not tell his family?" Clara asked.

"I can answer that. Wilmont Sawyer has never been easy on his sons as they grew up. In fact, Mark joined the military to get away from his father and prove to him he was not the loser Wilmont always said he was. I guess he couldn't face him after the dishonorable discharge."

"We have another problem. The bank closes in forty-five minutes. I have to get Brown and escort him to the bank to put a freeze on the account so Mark can't get to the money even online."

"If you freeze the account, he will have to go into the bank in person on Monday morning to find out why he can't withdraw the funds. Then you can catch him in the act, and I'm pretty sure Sally will be somewhere nearby to get her share before she makes her run for Europe."

"I'm out of here. I'm going to call the bank president to tell him I am on my way and why," the sheriff said. "I'll be in touch, Tammy. Great job."

They watched him speed away, leaving a trail of dust as he went.

"Have I ever told you how proud I am of you?" her aunt said.

"Many times, Aunt Clara, but I have never told you. I was so afraid when you vanished, but then I thought, she's Clara Beale, and no one can get the better of her. That kept me going and staying positive through the whole ordeal. You are a strong and feisty woman. I hope I have inherited the same gene and am just like you at your age."

"How about an early supper? We have much to discuss, that is, after you return from The Fry Shack with two big ole helpings of fish and chips and some sweet coleslaw on the side. You fly, I buy?"

"You never cease to amaze me," Tammy said, going inside for her car keys.

Over fish and chips, it was decided Clara would sell Idle Chat to Zee Campbell so she could open her hair salon. Her aunt would retire and do some traveling she had always wanted to do. The sale of the shop and surrounding land would give Clara's retirement account a hefty boost, and she could live comfortably and do all the things she had on her bucket list.

Her aunt dropped her fork when Tammy finally told her she was the one who bought the Grady mansion and was going to be staying in Braddock permanently. Her niece told her about wanting to start a writer's retreat at the mansion in the Fall when the surrounding mountains were showing off their peak colors. And maybe a week in December when the mansion was decorated in its finest Christmas attire.

Clara offered to do the cooking for the guests as long as she was home and not off traipsing around the world. She added that she could plan her trips around the retreats as she loved to cook for people and was darn good at it.

Zeke showed up in the middle of their early supper. He had come to take both women out to dinner to celebrate Clara's return but was too late. Tammy split her food with him, and Clara also threw a piece of fish his way. They caught him up on everything that had transpired during the day while he was at the airport, seeing his parents off.

"I still have a lot to tell the sheriff, but I think most of it will come out when he arrests Mark and Sally. I would love to be a fly on the wall when they are nailed at the bank. I do kind of feel bad for Wilmont in this whole mess. I know he's a jerk and all, but to have his son and his secretary pull this off right under his nose will be so embarrassing for him," Tammy said.

"I'll be on duty. I can tell you what happens when I get off at three."

"Or I can always go sit in the parking lot across from the bank and watch the whole thing for myself," Tammy suggested.

"No, they might spot you and take off. You promise me you will stay clear of the whole area," Zeke warned.

"When you put it that way, I promise."

"I'll make sure she stays right here and doesn't leave the cabin," Clara assured him.

"I can see the connection to the key on Sally's key ring, but how did you make the leap to them going after the money?" Zeke asked.

"Wilmont told me Sally told him I had paid three times as much as the taxes that were due in the first auction. Only the people at the closing would have known that information. Brown told his silent partner, and he, in turn, told Sally. I think originally, they were going after the existing money already in the account, and that's why they grabbed my aunt so early. The Grady money was a huge bonus, so they waited for the sale to be completed and the check to be deposited before they moved Aunt Clara to the bowling alley and made the anonymous call."

"You are one smart cookie," Zeke said. "Now I understand why your books are so good."

"Speaking of books, have you got any writing done while I was gone?" Clara asked.

"Some. I'm not going to lie; I should be further along than I am, but I will make up for it now that you are home," she answered, giving her aunt's hand a squeeze. "And wait until you see my new writing office at the mansion. It will be truly inspiring once it's finished."

"Trust me, it will. I have seen it," Zeke confirmed.

"Why don't you two grab a glass of wine or a beer or whatever it is you drink and head out to the porch? The weatherman said it was going to be a gorgeous sunset tonight," Aunt Clara suggested.

"Are you going to join us?" Zeke asked.

"Heavens no. This old lady is going to clean up the kitchen and then head to bed early. I still have some sleep to catch up on, and you two need some time alone."

"Are you sure? I can clean up," Tammy said.

"How difficult is it to throw away paper plates and disposable silverware? Honestly. Scoot and thank you both again for everything."

Her niece grabbed two glasses and a bottle of Zin. They spent the evening on the porch talking about the future, their future. Zeke left at ten to go home to let Blinky out. Tammy slid in between the cool sheets of her bed in the guest room and could hear the faint snoring of her aunt in the next room. The noise was comforting, and she was asleep in no time.

Keeping busy on Sunday, Tammy took her aunt to the ceramic shop. It was the first time she had been there since Goodwin Scott's death. The only difference was the color of the floor and a few fewer molds. Life had gone on.

Clara placed her hand on the closed cover of the large kiln. She whispered an apology to Goodwin and wished him peace in Heaven, telling him she would see him again someday in the future. She closed by asking him to be one of the ones who would meet her when it was her time to go.

An inventory needed to be done. The shop had to be emptied, so Tammy offered to make calls to various ceramic shops in the area to see if they wanted to buy anything at discounted prices. Zee told Clara there was no rush as her lease at the mall didn't expire until the end of September. This gave the two women the time to get everything done.

After finishing at the shop, they stopped at The Brown Bear café for supper. Zeke joined them, and Clara spent the whole time laughing at how much of a mess they made eating their Reubens. Zeke left right after supper as the next day was his first full day back at work since his assault, and he wanted to be well-rested to return to the job.

Tammy didn't sleep much. She feared something would go wrong, and the two would get away with the money never to be found. Three o'clock the next day seemed an eternity away.

Instead of sitting around watching the clock, Tammy shut herself in the guest bedroom and did some writing. She could hear her aunt humming happily in the kitchen while she baked some pies. The smell of the apple mixing with the cinnamon and other spices filled the house. Clara wanted something to offer Zeke when he came to deliver the news they were waiting to hear.

Four o'clock rolled around, and still, there was no Zeke. She shut down her computer and went to the kitchen, where her aunt was sitting at the table having a cup of tea.

"The water's still hot."

"Thanks. I wonder where Zeke is," she said, grabbing a tea bag out of the cupboard.

"I don't know, but I sure hope they got them," Clara stated.

They sat at the table, making small talk while watching the clock. A little after five, Zeke pulled into the driveway. Tammy and Clara were on the porch before he even got out of his truck.

"Well? Did you get them?" Clara asked.

"We did. Mark Sawyer entered the bank; he was furious he couldn't withdraw the money online. He demanded to see the manager who we replaced with one of our own. He was escorted into the manager's office, where we were waiting to arrest him."

"Was Sally with him?" Tammy asked.

"She was waiting in the car. We surrounded her, and she had no choice but to give up."

"It took so long to get here because of the interrogations. The sheriff questioned Sawyer, and I sat with Sally. Sawyer lawyered up right away."

"What about Sally?"

"She wasn't saying much of anything until I told her she would be charged with the murder of Goodwin Scott, and then she flipped on Mark Sawyer big time."

"I didn't understand why they murdered Goodwin. It didn't fit into the plan anywhere," Tammy said.

"It wasn't part of the plan. Goodwin was at the wrong place at the wrong time. He entered the shop to make his delivery not knowing that Mark was already in there. He looked up, recognized his friend from school, and called him by name. If anyone knew Mark had returned from overseas, the whole plan would unravel. He panicked and whacked Goodwin with the kiln shelf. Sally said he didn't mean to kill him, just knock him out. He was going to hide Goodwin at Sally's house, but when he saw he was dead, he stuffed him in the kiln instead."

"Is that where they hid me?" Clara asked. "At Sally's house?"

"Yes. You were kept in an empty butler's pantry, hence no windows."

"Whose idea was it? The plan, I mean."

"It was Sally's. She was eating at the diner and heard her brother sitting a few booths over, bragging to someone about the half million he had already collected from out-of-state investors for his housing development. Furious, she was trying to figure out a way to get the money from him and get even for all the money she lost."

"How did Mark become involved?"

"Mark had nowhere to stay, so he sneaked into the realty office and slept there, still having his keys to the place from when he worked there prior to entering the military. He was up and out early in the morning before anybody came to work. One morning, Sally came in earlier than usual and caught him there. She gave him the keys to her house and told him to stay there. That night, she offered him a way to get back into his father's good graces. If he went along with her idea, he would have enough money to give his dad back what he lost to Brown in the vineyard deal and still have enough left over to disappear somewhere and start again where no one knew him."

"And he went for it?" Clara asked.

"He did, but he changed his way of thinking. He wasn't going to give his father any of the money. Sally said they were going to go Europe together."

"Was it Sawyer who kidnapped my aunt?"

"He chloroformed her and carried her to the waiting car Sally was driving."

"So, Toby Brown had nothing to do with anything. The only thing he was guilty of was being a jerk," Tammy said. "Same as Wilmont."

"How did my sweater end up at the drive-in?" Clara asked.

"Mark put it there, that and the contract. He thought Brown owned the drive-in. He didn't know his dad had bought it a while ago."

"Just one more confusing element to the whole thing," Tammy stated.

"Speaking of Wilmont, he still loves Mark no matter what he has done. He hired a big-name attorney to defend his son against the murder charge."

"Brown gets to keep his money, and the only one who lost in this whole mess was Goodwin," Clara said, sighing. "It's not fair. He did nothing to deserve what happened to him."

"Don't you have a selectman's meeting coming up next Monday night?" Tammy asked her aunt.

"Yes, why?"

"Maybe you could bring up the idea of having a bench installed and dedicated to Goodwin in the courtyard behind the town hall. His mom works there, and she might enjoy sitting on the bench to visit with her son in the good weather."

"That's a great idea. I'll do it."

"How did Sawyer become Brown's silent partner if he had no money?"

"Sally fronted the money for Sawyer to use from her 401 K plan. She figured it was worth risking her fifty grand to get her hands on the investor's money already in the bank. Then, when Sally found out how much you bought the Grady place for, she delayed their theft of the money until they could have it all."

"They could have had over half a million and been long gone, but they got greedy," Tammy said.

"Who broke into my shop and smashed all the molds?" Clara asked.

"Mark Sawyer did that. With Brown being in the area a lot and harassing Hattie Cotton constantly, he figured everyone would point the finger at him."

"Just one more thing," Tammy said. "Who hit you and why?"

"Sawyer hit me. He thought I saw Sally coming out of the Flashpoint Realty office, and they couldn't take the chance I would have said something. Brown was away that day, so they thought they would be safe meeting at the office."

A knock sounded on the door. The neighbors from up the street were dropping off a casserole. Tammy watched her aunt greet her old friends and knew Clara would be okay. They were invited in for tea and pie. Declining, they cautioned Tammy to make sure her aunt rested, and she promised she would tie her down if need be. They said they would return at the end of the week for a visit.

"I haven't eaten today. I missed taking you ladies out to a celebratory supper last night, so what say we go out tonight," Zeke suggested.

"Truthfully, I just want to stay home, thank you. But that's not to say you two can't go out," Clara said.

"I don't want to leave you alone right now," Tammy replied.

"Pish! They got the bad guys, and I will be fine here by myself. Have been for years and will be now. Go, and when you come home, you can have some of my apple pie and coffee to finish the night."

"What do you say?" Zeke asked.

"I say lead me to the food."

They walked out to Zeke's truck hand in hand. He opened the door for her, and she climbed in. He smiled as he leaned into the open window.

"So, what do you think of our quiet, boring town now?"

"If this is quiet and boring, I'm going to love it here," she answered.

"And what about the company?"

"I think I'm going to like that, too."

"Just like?"

"Like will turn into something more, give it time," she replied.

"I got all the time in the world," he said, giving her a kiss on the cheek.

A Note from the Author

I am living a life-long dream of being a traditionally published author. Thank you, Summer Prescott, for believing in me and pushing me when I had given up on myself. Thank you, Cindy Bullard, for being the best agent ever!

Thank you, Shawn, at Level Best Books for believing in my writing.

Thank you to my three children, Meghan, Sarah, and Brandon, who have always supported me and have been my reason for living.

Never give up! I am sixty-five years old and am just now seeing a dream come true that started when I was eight years old and read my first Nancy Drew book.

About the Author

Donna's love for mysteries started at eight years old when she read her first Nancy Drew book. Her favorite genre is cozy mysteries, but she also loves to create spine-tingling thrillers and Christmas romances.

She is a member of Mystery Writers of America, Sisters in Crime, Sisters in Crime, N.E., and The Cape Cod Writer's Association.

Donna lives on Cape Cod, is happily divorced, has three grown children, and a rescue Papillon who rules the house.

SOCIAL MEDIA HANDLES:
https://www.amazon.com/stores/author/B00C401RS8/about
https://www.facebook.com/dwaloclancy
Donna Walo Clancy
Donna Clancy

AUTHOR WEBSITE:
www.donnaclancybooks.com

Also by Donna Clancy

Trash to Treasures Mysteries- Summer Prescott Books Publishing

Paint and Sip Mysteries- Summer Prescott Books Publishing

9 781685 125936